ENDURING RETRIBUTION

Aaron's Kiss Series Book 5

KATHI S. BARTON

WCP

World Castle Publishing
Pensacola, Florida

Copyright © by Kathi S. Barton 2012
ISBN: 9781938243042
First Edition World Castle Publishing February 14, 2012
http://www.worldcastlepublishing.com

Cover: Karen Fuller
Photo Shutterstock
Editor: Brieanna Robertson

CHAPTER ONE

Pete Marshall had a headache. She had been trying her best to talk with this man, well, the two of them, for the past two nights. And all she had for her effort was a throb between her eyes and was no closer to closing the deal than she had been before coming to this place. She reached for Dominic, her mate, knowing that he was at home and resting, as it was full light back there, but here in Paris, it was still night. In return, she felt him touch her, then he sent her warmth and took away the pain in her head. She sent him mental pictures of the naughty clothes she had purchased with him in mind just today.

"That isn't fair, love. You won't be home for another day and a half. And here I am with a raging hard-on, aching to be deep inside of you," he whispered through their mental link.

"Oh, Dominic, I miss you. I want you as well. Can't you come here by using that mind thingy like Tucker does? Just pop in my room and fuck me senseless?" She shifted in her seat. Damn she hated being away from him for so long.

"If that were possible, I'd be there now, but I can't materialize like that. Can't you cut your meeting short and leave tonight?"

He knew that she was there on business and that it was pack business. She worked as a security consultant for the largest pack in the United States with branches of businesses all over the world. Dominic was a bodyguard for Aaron and Colin, masters of their own realms, and they had asked that he stay and help out as they had to settle some major issues that had cropped up over the past few days. Otherwise, he'd be with her.

Dominic Marshall was a fair and honest man, taking his cue and all the help he could get from his best friend and master, Aaron MacManus. When Aaron and Colin had challenged and won a duel to the death to take over their respective realms, they inherited a mess, starving vampires without means to support themselves, internal problems within the ranks, and a stack of paperwork that would overwhelm any human, but this was multiplied by hundreds of years of neglect. There was money in the coffers, more than enough for them. It was just a matter of finding out the safest way to go about ensuring the best way to distribute it. Vampires didn't like change, and distrusted what they did not understand. It made for dangerous situations at times. Multiply that by all the pain and suffering they'd had to endure and it was little doubt there'd be problems.

"No, but I just might anyway. This man isn't listening to me, and I don't think he believes that Bradley has his best interest at heart."

Bradley Wolff, alpha leader to the pack she worked for, had asked her to go to France and help to get the security and software updated for the firm they owned, and to help them establish safer business practices. Nothing she said to the man was helping. She almost felt sorry for their translator, as she didn't speak French and Mr. Franco did not speak English.

"I love you, Pete. Hurry home to me."

She closed their connection. He was still there in the back of her mind. They could never break their connection as a bounded couple. She was glad for the gentle touch of him, now that she was so far away from him.

Pete felt someone move into her mind seconds before the person spoke. It was a gentle push, one to ask permission rather than invade and search, the mental way of calling on the phone.

"Yes? Hello?"

"The man, the translator, he is lying to you, to both of you. He's a danger to you." The voice speaking to her was low and urgent. Pete was suddenly afraid.

"How do you know? Where are you?" She reached out within the room and felt that every person had been blocked from her. *"Are you doing that?"*

"Yes. It's better if you just shut up and listen to me. Like I said, you're in danger with him. He is telling the man, the Italian that you're with, that you are a thief and mean to get into his data systems and steal from the pack. You are only approaching him to see if he would like a cut of the funds. You have done this work before and have yet to be caught; he's telling the other man. He told him that you are cocky and arrogant and though a beautiful

woman, you are still not to be trusted. I can believe the latter part myself."

"No, that's not right, he's French. I don't speak French. And I've never stolen anything in my life. I'm...wait! You know what he's saying? You're close enough to hear him." Pete wanted to look around, but was cautious.

"Because I understand Italian, because that is what they are speaking. I don't care if you've stolen or not. I'm telling you he plans to follow you back to your hotel and kill you in the name of the pack, whatever that means. Do you want my help or not? Because I could care less, lady. I have a job to do and you can be a sad consequence or not. I could care less."

"Show me who you are? How do I know that you're not going to do just what you say they are going to do?"

There was silence from the person, and she looked around the room again. Carefully, so as not to draw attention to herself, or maybe the person who was talking to her.

"Miss Larimore? Are you well? You seem...upset suddenly. Mr. Franco was just asking if you have any more samples of your work. He would like to see them." Pete looked at the man who spoke. Was he who he said or was the voice telling her the truth? Then she realized what he'd said.

"Oh, I'm so sorry, jet lag and all. Examples? No, I don't have examples of the security work, but you have the letter from Alpha Wolff. And I'm very good at what I do or Bradley wouldn't have sent me here to help you. If you'd like, you can call him yourself. But other than that, I don't know what else I can give you."

"This is what you should hear from him when he relays your question to Mr. Franco. In Italian. 'Amerebbe sapere che i campioni di altro o le dimostrazioni potrebbe mostrarla.' It means, 'She would like to know what other examples or demonstrations she could show you.' Oh, and that's in English."

"I understand English, thank you very much. Has anyone every pointed out how rude you are?" But she listened to Salvatore closely as he relayed her query. It was almost the same, but not quite.

"Amerebbe sapere che la prova di altro che lei ha bisogno di che può rubare il denaro con o senza lei. La potrebbe mostrare niente."

"That isn't the same, what did he say to him?" Pete noticed the slight differences, but not what it meant.

"Now you want my help. And yes, you aren't the first person to point out my one redeeming quality. He said, 'She would like to know what other proof you need, that she can steal the money with or without you. She could show you anything.' Are you willing to believe me now?" Pete could well imagine what someone might say. But she didn't have a choice. Not much of one anyway.

"Yes, it seems I have no choice. Oh, don't get me wrong, you haven't been all that trust inspiring, but you seem to talk a good game. Let me see who you are and I'll do whatever you want to make these guys pay."

"I have no intentions of taking your help, nor did I ask for it. I just wanted you to have a heads up just in case he slips away from me again. He's a slippery sucker, and

moves incredibly fast. He is using black magic, and he is very good at what he does. He has convinced Mr. Franco that someone named Bradley Alpha will reward him greatly for your death. And yes, before you ask, you are not the first this little man has tricked someone else into killing for him, all in the name of justice. You need to get out, right now. I can't protect you inside of here. You're too strong for me to hold along with everyone else. I want you to get out while you are still able."

Pete felt the door slam to the other person's mind seconds later. *Shit. Now what?* She couldn't reach for Dominic, as he would be crazy with terror for her safety. There were the two guards Bradley had insisted that she bring with her, but without causing a scene, she didn't know how to warn them that she was in danger. She looked around the room again and didn't see anyone out of the ordinary. *Shit and double shit.* Then she felt the person again. The touch was a little firmer, with maybe a little anger.

"One of them, the wolves with you, will meet you in the front hall, near the restaurant's main door; I just pushed him to move there. He doesn't know why he's where he is, but will wait, so tread carefully with him. I don't need a scene right now. The larger man, and sheesh, he is large, is in the bathroom and will be exiting very soon. Tag along with him to the front. He will look your way and it's up to you to go or not. Don't go back to your hotel. They know where it is. You'll be safe from there."

"How can I thank you? I don't...I would like to meet you in person. Please?"

"No." And the door shut again.

Pete could feel the mental lock the person—because from mental speak, you just couldn't tell the gender of someone—had slammed against her. She would get no more help from her. For some reason, she felt it was female. She looked up just in time to see Eon, her friend and body guard coming her way. When he looked at her, she motioned him to come to her, and she stood to leave, both men rising with her.

"Tell Mr. Franco that I'll get back with him in the morning. My head is just killing me and I'm going to go back to the hotel to take a strong sedative and sleep until morning. I appreciate your help, Salvatore. I'll see you tomorrow." *Over my dead body,* she thought as she hurriedly made her way to the front and out to the car. She hoped that it was just a figure of speech and not truth. Eon and Shawn were close around her.

~~~

Bailey made her way to the back of the restaurant just as Pete walked past her with her guards. She made sure the woman made it safely to her car, but not before the maitre d' stopped her to talk with her and for her to pay the bill. As a witness, he was ideal, if any was needed when this was all over. She had learned to cover her tracks over the years, and to get sloppy now would mean certain death. With that done, Bailey moved further to the back of the restaurant toward the table and the seat Pete had just vacated. On her way, Bailey pushed Mr. Franco into believing he needed to use the facilities. As he stood up to go, Bailey sat in the empty chair across from Salvatore.

"Hello, Salvatore, or is it Mark this time? Maybe you go by Thomas again. Oh! I know, Phillip, which was one of my all-time favorites, you know. Don't move. I have a gun pointed at your heartless chest under the table and I won't hesitate to kill you with it."

"You've been trying to kill me for months now, Ms. Lynne, but alas, I am smarter than you, a mere female. I will walk away again and you will go to your lonely bed to cry into your pillow." He glanced around for help, Bailey was sure of it. "Do you miss your dear Tyler? He was such a thrill to me. Sometimes just before I come in another deep ass, I think of his screams and I come all the harder for it. Yes, he was a tasty morsel." He licked his lips at the memory and to try and get a rise out of her as he looked around the room again.

Bailey had never been this close before. He'd always been one step ahead of her. But she wasn't letting him get away from her this time. He was hers and she had been chasing after his happy ass for months.

Her name wasn't Lynne, but a small variation on her real name. Very few people or beings knew it. Most everyone only knew her as The Printer, one of the most feared assassins of this and other realms around.

"Tyler's murder will be avenged, Salvatore. I'll see to that now. Enjoy hell as much as I'm going to enjoy sending you there."

And the gun went off, plowing twelve silver bullets into his chest and stomach. When she stood up, bringing the gun out from under the table, she pulled the trigger once more and shot him between the eyes, which were still opened in shock at the fact that she'd had the nerve to kill him. She made short work of removing his head from his body, her signature and a necessity in working with other beings, and after leaving the gruesome item on the table, she left the restaurant.

No one noticed what had happened, as she had held everyone in thrall for the few seconds it took to dispatch him to hell and for her to leave the restaurant. By the time she was halfway to the doors, she released everyone and mayhem broke loose, and just like that, the body had been discovered, not that it was easy to overlook—a severed head sitting in the middle of a table in one of the best restaurants in Paris. She had already taken care of the surveillance cameras here within the building and the ones along the street as well yesterday when she found out he would be there. Now she just needed to get the hell out.

Bailey walked into the street as she was tucking the once again fully locked and loaded Glock into her large bag. She slung it over her shoulder. Taking a deep breath, she started to step off the curb and into the street just as a large SUV screamed to a halt in front of her. Her gun was out and ready before the door closest to her opened. Even seeing who was there did not give her the feeling she could put it away.

"Get in. I know it was you and as I can feel everyone's panic inside. You must have caused the death of whoever they are screaming about, yet you're calm. I said to get in. Right now, the police are on their way."

Bailey looked down the street and saw two French police cruisers screaming around the corner, lights swinging across every building and the sirens echoing loudly. She didn't want to be caught in the crush of people being questioned about something only she knew about. So, with her gun still drawn, she stepped into the awaiting vehicle. They were moving down the street before Bailey had a chance to buckle her seat belt.

Bailey reached out to the driver and sent him directions to the nearest underground rail system entrance. She kept her weapon trained on the woman in front of her and didn't say a word as he careened around the corner to her destination. Keeping in his mind, she felt when someone else, presumably the woman across from her, reached into his mind as well.

Bailey felt the woman touch her mind then. Bailey could almost laugh at the frustration on her face, not that she blamed the woman, but Bailey wasn't going to be searched so easily. Bailey could speak several languages and what the woman was finding with her touch was four or five different ones scrambling around. Even if the woman could speak them, Bailey was simply reciting *War and Peace* word for word to her.

"You probably saved my life, but as someone has killed Salvatore, we will never know, will we? Why did you kill him? If you don't mind my asking, that is?" she asked her quietly.

"I don't know what you're talking about. Killed who?" Bailey never looked away, just kept staring at the woman as though looking for a sign or something.

She was actually. Just before anyone attacked, they always did one of three things: a) they tensed up just before; b) blinked several times so that they wouldn't when it was pinch time; c) made some sort of small movement to a partner. She knew these not because she had taken courses in human nature, but because she did observe people a great deal and watched what they did and how they reacted to different situations. Telltale signs had saved her life on more than one occasion. She was usually much too aware of her surroundings to be taken easily.

"Okay, we'll play it your way for the time being. But know this, I'm stronger, meaner, and much scarier when I want to be."

Damn it, Bailey thought just before sleep claimed her.

CHAPTER TWO

"Very good, Mac. Now, try this, open the door again, only this time I want you to focus solely on the woman from yesterday. Penny Gus, remember her? Focus."

Patrice Skidmore was enjoying the young boy's enthusiasm and barely contained excitement, Aaron observed. He was so serious one moment and a complete goof the next. When he and his twin got together, Aaron couldn't help but smile at their antics.

The lessons had been going on for a week now and Aaron was there every day watching the progress his son was making. They had found out only recently that he was a necromancer, and a very good one by all indications. He could talk to ghosts whenever they appeared, but mostly he'd had no control of them once they came. He hadn't learned how to put them back. Not a good term to use for returning the dead to their final resting place, but it was one Mac understood. So Mel, friend and queen of all magic, had recommended that they find him someone who could teach him control. That was why the lessons had begun. Having a power this strong and no control was dangerous to human and vampires.

Aaron looked over at the man seated at the makeshift desk. He was Tristan St. James the fifth, Patrice's oldest friend for almost four hundred years. Tristan hadn't looked up once from his laptop in all the time they had been there. Aaron grinned again, thinking about the look of complete horror on the younger vamp's face when Aaron had offered him the usage of his office while he was here. The mess on and around the desk nearly sent him into cardiac arrest, Aaron was sure. He'd tried to be polite, but finally broke down.

"How can you sit in here? It's a...you can't...oh my God, this is just nasty! There are papers everywhere!"

Aaron had known it was unorganized, but nasty? Well, he soon learned that anything that wasn't charted, pie graphed, and filed away was "nasty" to the man. He was the most organized, neat person he'd ever met. But that didn't stop Aaron from having fun at his expense.

"Really? Oh I don't know, I think it has a nice, homey look, don't you think?" Aaron said with all innocence.

Tristan didn't say a word, just snapped his mouth closed and walked away. He hadn't stepped one foot even in the direction of the room since. It was Duncan who had set up the table for him in the study, and had had Pete come over and hook up his Internet and modem for him before she had left for Paris. The top of the table looked as though he hadn't done a thing but sit there, but he'd been working every day since he came, brokering deals and buying and selling stock. He also designed and sold video games for different systems, and from all accounts, was very successful at it. Aaron watched him play with his children and knew that Tristan was getting ideas from them.

Patrice was more relaxed than her friend, which wasn't saying much; a steel rod was more relaxed than him. She was friendly, soft spoken, and polite. Aaron had thought there was some connection between her and Tristan, but was told they were just friends and nothing more. Aaron had thought that Patrice looked upset at that, but it was gone so quickly that he figured he had imagined it. The other day she had laughed at Tristan and ruffled his hair when he had suggested, well, ordered her to stop "flitting about" the house. She had been playing tag with the children and her laughter had been as loud as the children's. Tristan took more offense to her fluffing his hair than her laughing at him. The next time Aaron had seen him, he was back to his well-groomed self.

They were both members of the Royal House of Vampirism and the only purebred vampires anyone in this house had ever met. Tristan, as third son, was not required to have a bodyguard at all times, but as Patrice was the only daughter, and the youngest of five older brothers, she did have a bodyguard in the form of a brother, even a friend of a brother, as was the case now. One of them was with her at all times when she left the castle, no matter how much she complained about them smothering her, yet they stilled tagged along. Aaron didn't think there was anything wrong with this arrangement. Keeping an eye on the females of the world was just the way it should be done. But he had kept that comment to himself. He had learned a long time ago that Sara, his lifemate, didn't share the same views on that particular subject, and she was extremely good with a blade, thank you very much.

"We're all finished, Dad; can I go help Sam now?"

Mac had a big crush on Sam James, Tucker's mate, another vampire in his Kiss of friends and family. Sam was seven months pregnant and staying with them until their home was updated to vampire standards with underground lairs and such. She did most of the baking at her shop, Sam's Baked Goods, but experimented here in the kitchen when she had an idea. It worked out well for the ladies of the house, as they were all willing taste testers in these brainstorm sessions that happened nearly every week. Sam also baked the occasional un-birthday cake for one of the children at Becca's Place, and his own children at least twice a week. While Aaron didn't eat food of any kind, he very much enjoyed watching his mate's obvious enjoyment of it, especially cheeseburgers.

"Sure, son, did you thank Lady Skidmore? Good, run along now, and ask your mother to come in here, please?" Mac took off. Aaron noticed that Mac never walked when running could be done instead. When Sara came into the room, she was on the cell phone.

"But you don't know who she is? Yes, well, I can see that would be a problem. All right, just let us know what you find out. I love you too. Yes, I'll be sure to tell him. Good-bye."

"Pete has run into a slight problem in France. She will be coming home tonight and should be home sometime tomorrow afternoon. She may be bringing someone back with her. We'll talk more about it later."

Sara whispered through his mind, as she didn't discuss business in front of strangers.

"Is she all right? Nothing has happened to her, has it?" He was concerned about all the members of his Kiss, but he had asked Dominic, her mate, to stay here this trip as he had a large meeting with his advisors over the next two days, and he would never forgive himself if anything happened to her.

"She's fine, wonderful as a matter of fact. She said that she picked me up some beautiful negligees and that Dominic approved of hers and that you should like the ones for me just as much." Aaron felt her desire immediately, her body tensing with sudden need.

Aaron turned to Patrice when Sara sat on his lap. She hadn't actually started out there but on the seat next to him on the couch. But he couldn't seem to get enough of her. He needed to touch her whenever they were together whether there was company or not.

"Well, Lady Skidmore, how's he doing?" Aaron asked after he nibbled gently on Sara's neck

"He's a remarkable little boy. Mr. MacManus. He's smart, and willing to learn. He doesn't get easily frustrated when things don't go his way, like some other person I can name." She looked over at Tristan who just glared at her and resumed working. "He is very strong and in a few years will be able to call forth any soul and control it without problems."

"Why would he want to? I mean, why would there be a need for him to be able to call souls to him? I guess I don't understand what that sort of power can be used for."

Aaron understood that Mac was gifted, but was not sure how he would use this power.

Aaron knew that people, humans, considered vampires to be dead, the undead as a matter of fact, when in actuality they were as much living beings as anyone else. They just happened to need blood to sustain them rather than regular food. There were other creatures that needed emotions to survive.

"You're right, Mr. MacManus. It is an odd power, even for a vampire. But it will be useful in a great many incidents. For instance, as a vampire, he would be able to call forth a previous master and ask what had happened with this piece of property or why was this left unfinished…"

"Or why you left such a mess in my office," Tristan said in a low voice.

Aaron was sure Tristan hadn't meant to say it out loud because he flushed and shifted in his chair when Aaron looked his way.

"I doubt very much whether the previous master of this house even saw the mess on my desk. But if Mac happens to call him, I'll make sure he asks him for you." Aaron laughed again.

Tristan turned back to his computer. That's when Aaron noticed what Tristan had on his computer screen. It looked like his Lizzy as a cartoon.

"What are you up to there?" Aaron got up to have a closer look. "That looks just like my daughter."

"It is. Only in the game her name is Princess Elizabeth. There is her brother, Lord Maxwell, too." Suddenly, a caricature of Mac was on the screen. "I couldn't use their real names together so Mac decided on Maxwell."

They both watched as the children working together picked up the books and set them back on the shelf in a large study. The colors were brilliant and the children looked like they were enjoying themselves.

"I thought this would be a great way to teach children to plan and work together. There are problems to solve at every level that need to be thought out before they can move to the next level." When the room was cleaned up, bright balloons fell from the ceiling.

Aaron watched until the next problem popped up before he thought to ask, "But they aren't vamps, right? They're just regular children."

While he was sure that most people didn't believe in their kind, the few that did might find a way to put the two things together. Tristan assured him that they were just your plain old humans. Aaron loved what Tristan was doing and decided to talk to Pete about investing in some electronics like the ones needed to play the games that his kids played.

~~~

Bailey woke up about an hour after she'd been put to sleep in the van. She was lying on a bed in what looked to be a hotel room, a very big and expensive hotel room. She didn't give away that she was awake, but reached into the room and the one beyond and found that there was a woman, probably the one from the restaurant, and two men, the wolves, again, probably from the same place. She moved slowly just to make sure they hadn't done anything to her. When she found herself to be fine, she sat up on the edge of the bed and looked around. Her bag was lying on the floor next to the bed, so as she stood, she grabbed it and made her way to the bathroom.

She rummaged through the bag until she found her tooth brush, hair brush, and a tie to hold her hair back. She noticed that while her full magazines and clips to her guns where in there, the weapons, the two Glocks, were not. Also missing were the switchblades, taster, and the six cans of OC spray. She reached behind her to her lower back and felt the empty holster for the fourth hand gun, but found the one on her inner thigh was still strapped to her leg beneath her short skirt. This was a smaller version of the Glock, but just as deadly. Oh well, six shots were better than none any day of the week in her line of work.

Bailey Morrison was a bounty hunter, a damned good one too. She worked for anyone who could afford her price and had an excellent record. She seldom talked with clients, the transactions were conducted through the Internet, and money was wired to a dummy account. She owned her own firm, Fine Printings, Inc., a front of course, and it had worked for them all over the world. Her protector, Griff, a Celtic being called a Cynogriffon , worked with her as well, receiving and setting up any jobs that she did. She used to work with her brother Tyler until his death six months ago when Salvatore Madison had killed him in cold blood.

Tyler had been so happy just before he was killed, Bailey remembered. He had met the man of his dreams, someone he had thought to share his life with, he'd told her weeks before. Bailey hadn't had a chance to meet this mystery man, but was so happy for Tyler. When he had called her one night just a week before he was killed, saying that Salvatore wasn't what he seemed and that he was afraid for his life, she rushed home from Germany to protect him and to see what was wrong. He was dead before she could get to him, shot in the head execution style. The note Salvatore left for her said that he had served his purpose as a play thing and if Bailey wanted to have her back stroked by a master, try to find him. Salvatore had been difficult to corner until, about a month ago, she had finally thought to break through Tyler's secure work account. That was where she found all the information he had collected just before his death. She had enough evidence on just one of his murders that proved there needed to be a sanctioned hit on the man and she had contacted the Courts of Magick, her biggest client, to plead for one.

Tyler had found out that not only was he a murderer and a thief, but had been stealing for decades from various beings and humans. He had been acting as a translator for years, representing larger corporations to get inside information and then to kill one or both of the people who had hired him. He had recently been connected to the death of a man who had owned a large gaming company who had decided to branch out into other countries. The business man and his agent from France had been murdered, but the deaths had been made to look like a murder/suicide. It wasn't until Bailey arrived that they saw things differently. She had other information on similar deaths with the same details and MOs and had changed their minds. There had been a manhunt established right away, and because one of the men was a were, she was hired to find and terminate the bastard through the firm that she did most of her work for. She almost told them she'd do it for free, but hey, a girl had needs.

Bailey walked into the living room suite ten minutes later, refreshed but no less pissed off-looking. She had startled the younger of the two men, as he had been napping on the couch that barely held his large body and her opening the door with a slam against the wall had jerked him upright, but he remained where he was.

"Do you normally come into a room like that, or is it just for our benefit? Because I have to tell you, I'm not impressed. Childish behavior never has done so. I'm Pete Marshall, by the way."

Bailey looked over at the pretty woman. She was aware of Pete's magic. Bailey would have had to be stupid not to have. The sigil on the woman's face and arms also gave a good indication that she wasn't human.

"Just for you. I love to startle those that piss me off." Bailey moved further into the room. "There's a little matter of my weapons not being where I last saw them, like on my person. Would you mind returning them? I have another appointment to keep in a few hours and I'd like to have a bath, and a clean pair of underwear."

"Your guns are over there in the safe next to the couch. You can have them when you answer a few questions. Have a seat. I was just going to order some dinner and would be glad to order you some as well." Bailey stood.

The wolf on the couch shifted into a sitting position and the one near the other chair stood up as well. Bailey could have given Pete any detail she wanted about the room and the occupants without a single problem.

"No, not hungry, but I want you to open the safe. I saved your life, so to my way of thinking, you owe me, and I really have to go." Bailey braced herself as Pete stood. "So if you could hustle your ass over here and get it open, I'll be on my way."

"I was thinking of having a cheeseburger and fries. The guys are having steak, rare with all the trimmings. Of course the cherry pie won't be as good…"

Pete stopped talking when Bailey slid the chamber slide on the gun, her entire body tensed and poised for action. Bailey felt the anger and terror that quickly. One of the wolves started toward Bailey, but she stopped him with a look. Guns had that effect on people and she was sure he could smell the silver.

"Now," Bailey started again. "I've tried asking you nicely twice, so now we do this my way. Open the safe right now and I won't have to shoot any of you. Wolf boy?" The wolf on the couch looked up at her, a started expression on his face. "Yeah, I know what you are. Stand over there next to the wall with your back against it with your hands over your head and fingers linked behind your neck. Now you, hands up and fingers laced. Walk over to your brother and stand facing him with your right leg between his. That's it, all nice and cozy. Now if either of you move, one shot will kill you both. And I carry nothing but silver shot with silver casings and a liquid silver chaser, so no funny stuff. Now, Ms. Marshall, lets you and I lighten the load of this safe, shall we? And there will be no touching this time."

CHAPTER THREE

"I want this safe open. I want to get my weapons and leave." Bailey's gun was still pointed at Pete's head, and she was getting really tired of being threatened. Pete had contacted Aaron as soon as they had arrived at the hotel and had been told to bring the girl home with them. Fat chance of that happening now.

"I want to talk to you." Pete tried for bravado when in actuality, she was terrified. "I want to know why you killed Salvatore and why no one in that restaurant can remember you being there. It's been all over the news about his murder. I want answers, and I want them now. Then once I'm satisfied, you may have your guns and leave, but I can't let you leave before that. Salvatore was a were, and as a part of a pack, it is my responsibility to ensure his was a justified death."

Pete could feel the woman's anger. And her frustration. Well, Pete had enough of that as well. She wanted to be at home, not fighting some Amazon who was armed like Armageddon was coming and she was the sole protector.

"I've told you ten times now. I don't know what you are talking about. I was walking down the street and you offered me a ride. Had I known you were such a lunatic, I would have declined." Pete felt the gun press harder into her scalp. "Now you've robbed me of my things and won't return them. I have no problem shooting one of the men over there if that's what it will take to make you open this fucking safe."

"I know that you have great abilities with your mind. You held all of those people in that restaurant away from what you were doing until you left. I couldn't even penetrate your mind to find you and I'm pretty good at it." *Well,* Pete thought, *I thought I was good at it.* "I know you used one of the guns in your bag. I could smell the fire residue all over it when I picked it up. You're carrying no ID, so you are either hiding from something, or someone. There are changes of clothes in there and a locker key. Oh, by the way, we picked up the other bag you had there. Tricky how you put your things in different lockers all over the city. But once Shawn had your scent, it was easy to track down the rest of your things. I have all of those as well."

Pete watched her. She gave nothing away by sight or sound. Nor did the gun at her head waver. When Pete felt the touch in her mind, she knew it was the woman, and she let her.

"You're fucking nuts, you know that? Fine. Keep the shit. I'm making enough off this hit that I can replace what you've taken anyway."

Pete felt the gun leave her head and was relieved beyond imagining. But she couldn't let the woman go. Her

30

master had told her to bring her home. Leaping off the couch, Pete flew at the woman and knocked her to the floor. The gun skittered across the carpet, Pete was astride the fallen woman's back in seconds. She held her there with a mental body hold.

"Now, here is how this is going to work. You are coming with us. We are leaving this hotel and you are not going to give me a hard time about it. Are you even capable of not giving someone a hard time? Doubtful, I think." Pete felt a moment of fear when the woman beneath her moved. "You and I are going to go to the airport with Eon and Shawn, climb aboard the nice jet, and fly back to the States tonight. If you have somewhere to go, one last thing you have to do before we leave, then I suggest that you tell me right now. Otherwise, you are going to have to leave it for another time. I have your passport, well, all of them actually, and all your other information, Caitlynne Bailey, or whatever your name du jour is, and I will turn you over to the police if you make any sudden moves. Understand?"

"I want you to understand that as soon as I can, I'm going to fuck you up." And Pete believed her too, but hoped she wouldn't have the opportunity to do so.

Pete lifted Bailey's head by her hair and slammed it down on the floor hard enough for her to feel her teeth rattle. She didn't so much as whimper.

"I didn't ask you what you think you're going to do to me. I asked you if you understood me. Now, do you? Do you understand how this is going to work?"

"Fuck you!" And with that, the woman flipped Pete off her back and slammed her against the wall with what felt like a freight train. Before Pete could gather herself together, she was at her throat and had her held a good six or seven inches from the floor. It was then that Dominic touched her.

"Pete, what is it, what's going on?" She could hear the panic in his voice and knew that he was reacting to her pain and the anger running through her.

"Little busy right now, honey. Let me contact you later. Little problem with room service." She clamped her mind shut.

"I know I can't kill you," the woman breathed in her ear. "I can feel that, but I can put you in a world of hurt." She mentally push at her and tossed Pete across the room again and slammed her against the other wall. Pete looked to the two guards and saw that they'd be no help to her as the woman had somehow rendered them both unconscious and they lay in a heap on the floor. Pete knew she was so fucked.

Okay, enough was enough and Pete had had it. She summoned the power from the earth and threw it at Bailey. She had thought she'd move, and Pete had anticipated that too, just not where the woman had gone. The power hit her with enough force to knock her from the third story balcony door and to the street below.

Pete rushed to the broken door in time to see her hit, and hit hard, below her, blood pooling onto the pavement around her. Shit. Just her luck the stupid girl was standing in front of the door at that moment. Otherwise she would have simply hit the wall.

Pete did the only thing she could do; she reached for her master, and hoped that she hadn't killed the stupid woman.

"Aaron, is Tucker there? I need him in France, like ten minutes ago," she pleaded. Pain was starting to show itself to her in great big hurts. *"I've had...the woman is stronger than I thought and she just kicked my ass. But I think I hurt her. Badly. She needs blood now."*

"No, he isn't. What's going on, Pete? What's happened? Are you hurt, in danger?" Aaron asked.

"No. She's below on the courtyard. I can't...my vine didn't protect me from her. I don't understand." Pete looked down again. *"She needs a vamp, sire, or she's dead."*

"You mean the woman from the restaurant? I'm finding someone now, Pete." Pete could feel Sara close to Aaron, their combined magic almost palatable even through a mental link.

"Tell me what you know about her, Pete. Is she marked? Do you think that's why the vine didn't harm her?"

Pete didn't know how to answer Aaron. *"Honestly, I don't know. God, she's powerful, Aaron. She just threw me across the room like I weighed nothing, and she did something to the two wolves with me. I threw a power ball at her and she ended up on the pavement below my room. She's still alive, but I can't feed her. I...she hurt me. Not badly, but enough that I'm a little weak but all right. There's something about her, Aaron. I need someone here to heal her before she dies."*

She felt Aaron's comfort and strength as he sent it to her. *"Let me see what I can do. Just wait for a few minutes, all right?"* Pete could feel when another person of strength and magic entered the conversation, and wondered about it.

Pete didn't answer about the sigil, hers or the woman's. Pete didn't know why hers didn't hurt the woman, and she had no idea if the girl had one or not. This was a very strange night, she decided.

Pete was a wood nymph and she was marked as such. Her mother, part Fae, had mated with a nymph and Pete had been born of that union. Pete's mark had protected her and Dominic, her mate, when they had needed it, but it hadn't with the girl.

The vine, a beautiful work of art of thick ivy, covered most of her body and down her arms and legs. Pete's face was covered in green leaves and looked like a very well done tattoo to humans and some beings alike. Whenever Pete or Dominic had become threatened, the vines would cover them protectively and hurt, even kill those that caused them harm.

"Tristan can materialize anywhere over long distances. I can only manage short hops and it will take too long for me to get there," Aaron told her. *"He is leaving now."*

"Thank you, master. I will explain when I get back home. Please tell Dominic that I'll be there soon and that I'm all right."

Pete felt him laugh. *"I'll try, young lady, but you had better be bringing him back something naughty to appease him with. You know how he can be."*

Pete snorted. All the vamps she knew, and some wolves, were very worrisome. She wouldn't be surprised if they all met her at the airport.

~~~

To say Pete was surprised would have been an understatement, if the look on her face was any indication, Tristan thought. One minute she was begging Aaron for help, the next there stood a strange vampire in her room. Tristan was slightly surprised to find the woman looking so pale.

"Oh thank goodness, she's down here," Pete said in way of greeting. "I hit her with a power ball and knocked her out the door. The ball goes to what I want it to, and will track. And since she didn't have the good sense to just cooperate with me in the first place, when she ran in front of the door, bang! The sucker got her."

Pete was moving at vampire speed down the stairs toward the back of the hotel. Tristan was close behind. Pete was babbling, but it was a nervous babble, one that said she was scared that he might not be able to save her. Tristan didn't know why this injured woman was so important to them, but he would do what he could.

Tristan stopped ten feet from the girl who lay broken on the grass. He could smell her blood and feel her immense pain. She was breathing, but just barely. Her pulse had slowed and she was losing blood much too fast. He could also smell another scent, one that was unique to him, daisies and sunshine. And it was everything Tristan could do not to turn around and go back to the States and forget he'd ever decided to help Aaron.

What were the chances of finding his mate while helping out someone, a master someone at that? He lived in France most of the time, having been born there, so finding his mate there while visiting the States was too much to bear. He didn't want to settle down, not now, maybe not even ever. But he had given his word he'd help out. Aaron MacManus was a good man and good men were few and far between. Especially vampires.

Tristan slowly walked to her and knelt down. He searched her body mentally and found that if Pete hadn't have acted when she had, the woman would indeed be dead. Her back was broken, as were both her legs. She had eight ribs broken and one had punctured her lung. Her left hip was also broken in two places. Her jaw was cracked and she had a deep concussion. Plus, there were a multitude of cuts and abrasions, glass still imbedded into several of them. Tristan opened the vein at his wrist and forced her mouth open with his other hand. He squeezed her nose closed so she would either have to swallow or choke. He knew what he was doing, and the consequences of his actions. As soon as she swallowed the first mouthful, it was sealed. He was halfway to fully bonding with her, and he wasn't happy about it.

When a pureblood bonded with a mate, it was slightly different than a turned mating. There had to be a blood exchange, a give and take at the same time. There also needed to be a sexual completion for them both, preferable with another blood exchange to ensure the bond. Once that was complete, they would be truly bonded and mated. But Tristan was of royal blood too. With this, there was a ceremony where they used a family heirloom, a jeweled dagger, and cut a vein over their hearts and drank from there. This exchange was more of a ritual than a need, but it was still practiced today. But he didn't want to think about that right now. Besides, maybe, just maybe, he was wrong about the girl. And she was just a woman who smelled good. *Yeah,* he thought, *and I'll go do a jig in the sunny streets tomorrow afternoon.*

He felt Pete standing over him moments later. He didn't take his eyes from the woman on the ground who was still sipping from his wrist. He didn't have to hold her nose any longer, as she was now drinking greedily from him. The taste of him to her was just as addictive as her scent was to him.

"Who is...do you know her name?" he asked Pete, who stood just behind him. He could feel that she had just fed. His own hunger leapt in response to her fresh smell.

"She didn't have any ID on her that we could use, but we managed to track down seven lockers at different points across the city. Each one had a different passport and identification to go with it. There were several variations on the same names, but nothing solid. She...she saved my life tonight. It's my fault she's in the condition she's in. I...her power base is incredible."

Tristan didn't say anything for a long time. He pulled away from her mouth and licked the wound to seal it. She was badly hurt still. His blood, being pure, would heal her, but it would take a while because of the extensive damage that had been done to her. But she wouldn't die, not now at any rate.

"She can't be moved yet, at least not by conventional means. I have a place here in the city we can all go to. I'll take her with me and you and your men can meet us there. I'm Tristan St. James, by the way, and you are…"

"Sorry, I'm Piccadilly Marshall, everyone calls me Pete. I'm mated to Dominic, Aaron and Colin's bodyguard. I have to get back to the States soon. My mate is nearly bonkers without me, and he knows, you see, about tonight. He wants me home."

"Understandable. I will take the young woman with me then and will contact Aaron when she is able to move on her own. I will send someone for her things, if that is acceptable to you. Is there anything you can tell me about her? What she was doing in Paris?"

Not that it mattered, really. Aaron had sent him to Paris to save the young girl, and that he'd done. Whatever else happened was going to be all on Tristan.

"Yes, of course, I'll have everything ready when they come. She is armed, or was. I've never seen so many weapons on one person in my life. She had two, no, three guns, a couple of lethal-looking blades, switchblades I guess, a tazer, and a few cans of really strong pepper spray on her. Inside of the lockers were more guns and ammo, even a few sticks of dynamite in one of them. Each one of the identifications we found has a permit to carry a weapon with it. She's powerful, as I've said, but I don't know what she is."

Pete hesitated and Tristan was almost afraid for her to continue. "How did you meet her? I mean, if you fought, I can only assume you didn't know her from before."

Tristan felt one of the guests from the hotel start to come out onto the patio just in front of them. He sent him away with the thought to make love to his wife instead.

38

Humans needed the comfort of touch and Tristan was merely giving it to him. Besides, they didn't need any more witnesses to this.

"She warned me that I was in trouble and that the man I was using as a translator had been lying to me. She was able to hold an entire restaurant in thrall while she shot, killed, and beheaded a man without being noticed. I have since found out that there was a warrant out for his arrest. He was considered armed and dangerous. And according to my source, police were to shoot on site. I don't know how she managed to get the jump on him, as she had made sure I was safely out before she did it. Oh, and she speaks Italian. Very well, as a matter of fact. As for being in Paris, I don't know for sure. I'm sure it had something to do with the man from tonight."

Tristan merely nodded. He was still trying to figure out what to do about her and had only heard about half of what Pete had told him. He was still trying to come to grips with what the woman was to him. And also what he was going to do about it.

"Tristan, I'd be very careful when she wakes up. She is a mite demanding. And she can be rude when the mood suits her, which seemed a great deal of the time." He heard the laughter and the seriousness in her voice and wondered about it.

"Yes, I will, but she won't be able to hurt me. Thank you, Pete. I'll be taking her now." He reached down and picked Bailey up, cradling her in his arms tightly. He dematerialized both of them away seconds later.

~~~

It wasn't until a man who identified himself as Anthony, second butler to the St. James household, had gathered the girl's four bags and drove away that Pete finally understood what Tristan meant. The woman he had just saved, the woman who she had almost killed, was his mate. Pete nearly laughed herself into a stupor all the way home and wondered often what she smelled like to him.

CHAPTER FOUR

Bailey woke up in a dark room. She started to move to get up when a searing pain rushed through her body, a moan escaping before she could stop it. She reached out and found that she wasn't alone in the room. There was a vamp in the room with her. A male.

"The pain will lessen in a few hours. Then it will be gone altogether very soon, I would guess. Would you like some help getting up?" The voice was across the room, which was too dark for her to make out just where or who the voice was.

"Where am I?" She moved again, slower this time, and finally got her legs off the side of the big bed. She sat still, fighting against the overwhelming pain so that she wouldn't pass out, but she really had to work at it.

"Impressive, young lady. You must hurt very badly right now. I wouldn't have thought that there was any way for you to move much less sit up for several more days. My son brought you here yesterday. You were damaged very badly. Cover your eyes and I'll turn on a few lights." The voice had a hint of humor, and class.

Bailey couldn't have lifted her hands to cover her eyes if her very life depended on it, so she just closed them tightly against the sudden glare, and even that hurt some. After a few moments, she opened them a little at a time until she could see again. She gently turned her head to where she thought the man had been sitting and sucked in her breath. There sat the most handsome man she'd ever seen. She looked away. Men like him made her nervous. Actually, all men did.

"Damaged? You said I was damaged, what does that mean? And how did I get here? The last thing I remember was fighting some she bitch in a hotel in Paris."

"Yes, I'm sorry, I meant to say injured. Humans are injured, my kind is damaged. The bitch, ah, that would be Pete Marshall, I assume. She called her master and he sent my son as he is able to move through space very quickly and was there visiting. He healed you and brought you here to mend, err heal. You are still in Paris, in our home. It's Tristan's home actually."

"I don't know...Tristan? I don't know him, unless he's one of the people hanging out with this Marshall chick."

"No, no, Tristan is a vampire, a pure blooded one at that, and as I said, my son. He should be returning soon. He needed to make a quick...he was thirsty, you see." *Thirsty, good thing to call sucking the life out of someone,* she thought.

She finally stood up, swayed slightly, and would have fallen if he hadn't flashed to her side to catch her. Before she could think, she jerked from him and cried out as the pain again tore through her. As she was falling into a black void to escape the pain, she heard someone yell out. She didn't think it was her, nor the man she'd been talking to, though it was definitely the voice of a male.

This time, when she woke up, Bailey took a survey of herself and the room before she moved. The pain was manageable, barely. Bailey reached out into the room and found a female sitting in the chair this time. She didn't bother with conversation. She could feel the woman's gentle probe into her mind. Bailey knew she wouldn't get much, just what she wanted her to have. Bailey managed to turn over and sit up before the woman spoke.

"My name is Abby St. James, and you are?" The room brightened with candlelight in gentle increments, instead of the flare of overhead lights. Bailey knew immediately this room was different than the one before. It was darker and there were no windows.

Instead of answering, Bailey wanted her things. "I had some stuff. The other woman, the one from the hotel, said she got it all. I'd like it please."

"I believe it's all here with the exception of your arsenal. Tristan has taken that to the safe in the other wing of the house. There are clean towels and a new toothbrush in the bathroom. I'll wait here, and then we'll talk."

"Whatever."

Bailey hobbled to the beautifully appointed bathroom. It was as big as most hotel rooms she stayed in when working. Of course she tended to stay in dives, but still, it was huge. The double vanity was the length of the room, about ten feet. There were high gloss cobalt pottery bowls sitting under the long necked faucets instead of sinks. The lights around the mirrors were soft and reset into the wall behind them. There was a deep pool, not a tub but an actual pool with a water fall coming from somewhere above with plants hanging from different heights. When Bailey ran her hand through the water, she found it to be very warm, almost hot and smooth. Unlit candles surrounded the pool, sitting on rocks and nestled in plants. Next to it was a shower stall that four people could easily stand in, with jets at different levels and overhead. As much as she wanted to strip down and sink down in the pool, she reached into the shower and turned on the water. The sooner she was out of here, the better.

Fifteen minutes later, she walked out of the bathroom. The aches and pains had lessened to the point where she didn't limp. And if need be, and it would have to be a big fucking need, she could defend herself. Her hair, always a pain most times, had cooperated and was now pulled back into a tight French braid that hung damp past her hips. The woman, as promised, was still waiting for her.

"I need to leave. While I appreciate your hospitality, I will be going." Bailey began gathering her things up and setting them on the chair next to the big bed.

There wasn't a bag, but her pants gave her enough places to stash things so she wasn't overly concerned. Clips went into various pockets, the blades clipped to her belt, as did two of the OC spray canisters. The rest of her gear fit into hidden pockets here and there throughout her clothing. The woman, Abby, she'd called herself, hadn't said a word.

The woman had to see that Bailey was neither nice nor human. She was defiant and strong, incredibly so. Bailey also knew she should have been out for another couple of days at least, but here she was, a mere twenty-four hours after having been thrown from a third story balcony, making demands and expected them to be granted.

"This Tristan person, do you think he'll let me get my stuff later? I have things to do today and I don't have time to wait on him while he drains some unsuspecting woman. Or man if he's into all that." Bailey knew enough about vamps to know they liked sex with their dinner. Sort of like a meal and a show, she supposed.

"Have a seat, please. I believe you and I have some things to discuss. I don't have your guns, as I've said, so you'd have to wait for Tristan to return to get those anyway, so you might as well relax for a while." Abby indicated the chair across from her before she smiled and continued. "You didn't tell me your name."

"No, I didn't. Sorry, lady, but I don't do social. Night." With a flick of power, Abby St. James slumped in her chair.

Bailey found her things laid out in very neat piles on the table in the room. Everything was clean and folded in pristine order, stacked, and smelling fresh. Her shirts, all black and all t-shirts, were lying on top of her jeans, also all black. Her socks, which she had never mated together, the only reason why she always bought the same kind, were not only folded by pairs but stacked end to end. Her panties and bras, the only real things she spent any money on, were spread out, not rolled up, as if the person who put them there was trying to see how they would look on someone. *Whatever*, she thought with a mental shrug. Her other items, toiletries, passports, all seven of them, were put into pile of use, bathroom stuff all together, purse stuff, if she bothered to carry one, together. She simply reached out, grabbed one of the biggest bags she carried, and scooped it all into it without a thought to how messy it would be again. Stuff was stuff, and who cared what it looked like so long as it covered what it needed to and was clean?

It took her about twenty minutes to navigate the sub levels. She discovered why there was a pool; they were below ground a good ways and deep into a cavelike structure. After she had had to back track twice, she finally made her way to a set of narrow stairs and up to the main floor. She reached into this level and felt that there wasn't anyone about in this part of the house. And from what she could feel, the house was massive.

She managed to leave the house and the grounds without anyone seeing her. She knew that the outside security cameras would pick her up, but there was little to nothing she could do about that without more time. She was able to disengage the gate, and then rearmed it. She wouldn't leave them vulnerable just because they had pissed her off. She shifted and flew into town.

Bailey was standing in line at the check-in counter at the airport gate when her cell phone sounded. It was such an unusual event that it took her a few rings and someone to poke her from behind for her to realize it was her ringing. She answered it on the final ring, and as soon as she heard the voice, wished that she had left it to go to voicemail.

"Hello?"

"I have another job for you. This one is in Germany. When can you get there?"

Neither of them used names. The phone was a pay as you go so that there were no bills. Also, since she traded the thing out at random intervals, it was nearly impossible to trace to her.

"I can be there in six hours, provided you pay for the last job before I purchase my tickets. The stationery was delivered over twenty-four hours ago, and we have cash on delivery billing in our business, remember?"

She hated working for people who didn't follow rules. Bailey liked rules and liked them even better when they went her way. She snickered at the thought.

"The money will be wired in one hour. This job is a rush and I'm willing to pay you for any set up fees. And a bonus if you can have it printed in less than ten hours."

The voice was never the same, but she still kept notes on the words or phrases that were used each time. This particular voice was one that she'd talked to over a dozen time and the targets were always human who had let the dark magic or black get the better of them and had taken lives. Bailey wasn't sure why, but she didn't wholly trust the person at the other end, hadn't from the very beginning. There was something just off about it.

"No. Now. I have to pay my employees, and I don't work that way. I believe we've had this same conversation about a dozen times now."

Bailey hung up. They'd either call her back or wire the money. She really didn't care which. When she got to the ticket counter, she purchased a ticket for the next flight to Rome. Once there, she would go to Germany if the bill got paid in a timely manner. Bailey didn't think about the time factor. Never take a direct route when several would get her there safely and keep her ass safe. She always used cash too. Covering her tracks wasn't just a concept, but a way of life for her.

Everyone, including her and Griff, always used printing terms when they called. She didn't have the first clue how to print anything and even if she was to use a copier, she'd have to get out the manual to see how to turn one on. It seemed a good plan at the beginning. Griff, Tyler and she had laughed for hours about how someone would call in and ask for a hit. It had gotten so ridiculous that when they were approached the first time by their first client a few days later, they nearly lost the job because they couldn't stop laughing. She had been ten years old. And keeping the humans at bay had gotten to be easier all the time.

Bailey's phone rang just as she was being called to be seated. It had been only seven minutes since she'd told the voice to pay or fuck off and two since she had been notified by Griff that the money was in their account. With a grin, she answered.

"I just checked, and we are good to go. I'll call you when the next job is received." She hung up. She didn't leave any chance that he could trace the calls. It was hard to do on the type of phone she used, but it could be done. And at the rate things were going with technology, that too would be a way of the past. Bailey took the battery out of her phone and crushed it in her hand. Then she snapped the phone in half and dropped the two different pieces of it into two different trash cans along the tarmac.

Bailey made a very good living at what she did. If she stopped working right now, she'd have enough money to live very nicely for the rest of her days. The excitement of the job and doing it well had gone out of it with the death of Tyler, though. He had been everything to her; maybe, she thought, it was time to hang up her guns. And just as that thought entered her mind, she pushed it away. She couldn't quit, not right now, maybe not ever.

Tyler Dunn hadn't really been her brother. They had been closer than that, if possible. They had met in the lab at Co-Tech Industries. They had both been lab experiments. He had been born a wolf and sold to the company when he was still a cub; he'd been about eight weeks old. Then his parents, for whatever reason, had just never returned.

The techs had thought to change him into the perfect killing machine by injecting steroids and other nasty chemicals into him. But they hadn't counted on him being soft hearted. Without the drive or natural inclination to kill, his size and abilities aside, he would be useless to them.

Bailey had been six years old then to his eight. She had heard that they were going to "dispose" of her friend for noncompliance and she'd stepped in to save him. She found him drugged and tied up in a cell. They had all escaped. She had been there since conception, being a creation from a test tube, so knowing just how to get out was easy for her. She too had been set up for termination, her flaw of mortality rendering her useless as a candidate for the elite killing squad.

Griff, a Cynogriffon, had been in the cell between hers and Tyler's, and he had pledged his immortal life to her if she took him with them. They did, taking the man to

Tyler's left as well. Charlie, another creation like her, had been shot as they were making their way across the compound. He took a bullet intended for her.

Griff had been a donor, a sperm donor to their test tube creations. He had also been their best trainer when they needed a sparring partner to their soldiers. Griff was a beautiful and fierce creature, and being an immortal, a perfect candidate for what they needed. They used him for his abilities that he could pass on through his sperm, which made him invaluable to them.

They had lived by their wits and abilities, nearly starving to death the first year. Bailey would devise a plan and Tyler would figure out the logistics of it and Griff would protect them from afar with his powerful magic. They rarely got caught, and when they did, Bailey would "shadow" them out. Her powers got stronger as she got older. It wasn't until she was eleven or twelve that she figured out she was able to shift, to change into whatever she wanted. Her shifting and Tyler's seven-foot, eight-inch bulky frame had helped them get their first job accomplished. A vampire gone rogue was not an easy kill.

When Bailey finally boarded the plane to Rome some forty minutes later, she found herself seated next to a chatty woman and her young son. The boy was annoying, as was the woman with her constant yelling at Paul. Within an hour of taking off, Bailey put them both into a deep sleep. Bailey herself slept well for the first time in days.

CHAPTER FIVE

Tristan hung up the phone and started breathing deep, in and out, in and out. He'd never been so angry in his entire life. She had actually knocked his mother out. Of course, Mom thought it was funny and intriguing to say the least. One minute she was telling her what was what, and the next, poof, waking up several hours later. He wondered how she would feel about the young lady if she knew he refused to mate with her. By the time she woke again, the girl had left, taking her clothes and leaving the passports behind with a note.

'Thanks for your lovely hospitality; I have never enjoyed a more friendly stay in my life. I won't need these anymore as they've been compromised. Have a nice life.'

And no signature, not even initials. Damn her.

Tristan closed his eyes and reached for her. He had given her his blood, quite a bit, as a matter of fact, so finding her shouldn't be a problem. He frowned; she was far, no longer in Paris, but…Germany. What the fuck was she doing in Germany? He stretched farther and found her running, running from someone. She was in danger and angry. He stiffened when he felt the first bullet enter her, the pain searing through her, then a second one. Still she ran, stumbling now. When she lost conciseness, he lost his connection with her. He found himself standing, ready to…to do what, he didn't know, but he knew that she was in trouble, the little fool.

Tristan found Aaron in his study and told him that he was needed elsewhere for a few days, would he mind keeping an eye on Patrice?

Aaron just laughed and agreed to help him out. "I don't suppose this has anything to do with the woman in Paris, does it? Pete said she's a mean little thing."

"It is, although I don't know what could be so funny about it. I've only known her for a short time and she's been in more trouble than I have had in all my life." Tristan picked up his briefcase.

He kept it as close to him as most men did their wallet. Probably more so if he had to hazard a guess. Straightening his tie, he was ready to leave. "She's my mate. I don't want her to be, but there you have it. What am I supposed to do with her, I ask you? Why, I don't even know what she is much less her proper name."

"Not much you can do now that you've found her." Aaron grinned at him as he offered up a suggestion. "I would suggest that you try talking to her. From what I've heard, she isn't too happy when she's pushed."

Tristan thought that was an understatement and he left the building to find her. She was going to have to learn some ground rules. Somehow, though, he didn't think she was going to like that any better than being pushed.

Tristan hid in shadows when he got to the place of their last contact. There was police tape encircling the area where she went down and the police were still milling about. Her blood was in a dark pool within the tape and his only means of finding her. It took him an hour to track her scent from the blood, as he had never tasted hers before and that made it slightly more difficult. She was still alive and currently in a local hospital, the officer told him. He hadn't actually told Tristan, but it was in his mind. The officer also thought she was very beautiful. For reasons Tristan didn't want to think about, that pissed him off royally. He materialized there next.

Staying shadowed, Tristan went into her room, having followed her scent to the correct one. She had a policewoman in the room with her, and was handcuffed to the bed by her right ankle. Her arm was tied down by a soft cloth restraint with an IV in the back of her hand. There was bleeding a little from her surgery and there were staples holding the wound closed. Her left leg was propped up with a pillow and wrapped up as well. He could smell the gun residue there. She was still sedated, but only slightly now, having come from surgery an hour ago.

Tristan pushed the officer into going out of the room with the need for a smoke break. Tristan could smell the tobacco scent all over the woman. He could also smell the beginnings of lung cancer, and promised himself when she returned he would stop her need for the nicotine once and for all. *Stupid humans.*

He stood over her for a few minutes just looking at her. This was only the second time he had seen her if he didn't count taking her to his home in Paris, and the both times she had been unconscious. He'd have to claim her soon if he wanted to spend any time with her. At this rate, she wouldn't last very long the way she got into trouble. It didn't occur to him that he was planning their future and would have denied it if he'd been asked.

Putting his wrist to his mouth, he opened his vein for her again and put it to her mouth. She resisted harder this time, her body not as broken, nor near death, but finally gave in and drew him in when he closed off her nose again. He only gave her a few sips, not wanting to alarm anyone with her miraculous recovery. Once he sealed the tiny opening with his saliva, he studied her. She really was very beautiful.

Her hair had been put into a haphazard knot on top of her head, and its rich fall colors brightened against the white of the pillow. Her face was oval-shaped with brows that were perfectly shaped, arched just enough. Her nose was small and sloped with a small bump in the middle where it may have been broken once and knowing what little he did of her, probably more than that. Her mouth called to him with its fullness and shape. It begged for kisses, deep, exploratory ones, and he wanted to do just that. Her jaw was strong and stubborn-looking, which in light of recent events, was probably as true a statement as anything else. Her right shoulder was bare, allowing for the wires from the heart monitor and other equipment to do their work. It begged to be bitten. He found himself leaning down to give in to temptation and brushed his lips across hers. He moaned aloud, her taste exquisite, her breath warm. He ran his tongue along her jaw and then down the long column of her neck. He paused over her pulse. Feeling it beat against his tongue sent tremors throughout his body, centralizing at his cock. He needed to taste her, he justified to himself, so that he could find her quicker if she needed him, when she needed him, he amended. Just a taste, just to find her. Even as he bit, he knew it for the lie it was.

His cock surged at her taste when her blood entered his mouth, his need to be inside of her blotting out everything around him. He drew deep from her, her essences filling him, completing him. He rubbed his hand hard against his cock, hoping for some relief of the sudden and overriding need to come, but to come deep inside of her. She moaned and he felt it as surely as he tasted her. Suddenly, he heard the voices just outside of her room seconds before he gave in and pulled his cock free to…he wasn't sure what his plan had been. It was as though he had been jolted awake from a dream that he didn't know how would end. Panting hard and aching, he sealed the wound to her throat and pulled back into the wall just as her door opened.

"No, I don't know who she is. As I have said numerous times already, she had no identification on her at the time we found her body."

Two men entered her room, oblivious to Tristan only a few feet from them. Luckily, he understood enough German to know what they were saying, as it was his second language.

"So, let me get this straight, because if I'm hearing you correctly, you were chasing a man who had shot and killed another man and ran across this woman lying there bleeding. Is that about right? She was just lying there with nothing on her, not even a purse or anything?" The detective growled low in his throat. Tristan could feel that he hated the other man, really and truly hated him. Touching the other man's mind, Tristan could see why. The man was by and far the most stupid man he'd ever known and quite possibly the most incompetent.

"Yes, that's what I'm telling you. If you want my opinion, I think that…"

"I'm not paying you to think, you fuck wad. I'm paying you to catch the bad guys. Does this little bit of a thing look like a bad guy to you? Hell, my wife won't go to the fucking mail box without her purse. Let me tell you what happened. She was in the wrong place at the wrong time. That's all. Whoever you were chasing took her purse and shot her when she made a noise. Understand me? I want you to take these cuffs off of her. Leave the guard. Poor mite, he has her address and things so I want her safe."

"I…she's my wife. I can protect her. The officer, I won't need her. I have my own bodyguards for her safety." Tristan stepped out of the corner and was talking before his mind knew what the hell his mouth was doing.

Both men jerked around at the voice behind them. Neither man had known that he was in the room, and they wouldn't have until he was ready. Tristan was trying to think fast. He'd never been much for lying and had thought he was really terrible at it.

"I'm sorry, Mister…?"

"St. James. Tristan St. James. This is my wife…err what happened? I…when she didn't come home, I called a few of her friends and they told me where she had gone after lunch. I followed her...I looked that way and found the crime scene tape and came to the hospital. They told me they had a Jane Doe fitting her description and it's her. My wife, that's her." He sounded like a moron, he thought.

He looked over at her at that moment and saw that she was looking at him. His breath caught in his throat. The moan he just barely caught before it had escaped was frozen in place. Her eyes, they were...well, green just didn't do justice to the color, and hers were radiant. Emeralds were the first thing he thought of then dismissed that as well. They paled in comparison to the beauty that now glared at him.

"Your wife, huh? If I'm your wife, you should at least show some concern that I'm awake, shouldn't you, honeybunches?" Tristan didn't like her tone, nor, for that matter, her calling him names.

"Are you going to play along, or do I let them know that you aren't as innocent as they think? Because by accounts, there is no way you fit the 'poor mite' description either."

"Hummm, good point, but what makes you think I'm not innocent? The ball is in your park, bloodsucker. What do you wanna do? If you leave, I can make sure they never knew you were here. And in actuality, I'd prefer that you did leave. Shoo." Tristan felt the strong compulsion in her voice and had to work hard at ignoring it.

He didn't know whether to laugh at her or to spank her. No one had ever "shoo-ed" him before and he was reasonably sure that he didn't like that either. He decided to set her straight on a few things.

"My name is Tristan, not honeybunches, or bloodsucker, if you don't mind. I absolutely hate pet names. And I'll play this out for now, if you behave, or is that not within your scope of understanding?"

"Fuck off, dick weed." She spoke out loud next, putting as much pain and agony in her voice as she could. Tristan didn't think he could stomach much more so was glad when she only did it for a minute.

"Sweetums, is that you? Oh my, love buckets, I've had such a horrible experience. I was so frightened. That man, he was so bossy to me. You know how I hate to be yelled at, doddle butt, and he was so beastly to me." She gave a little sob and a sniffle.

"Stop calling me those ridiculous names! And don't quit your day job, you're a horrible actress. By the way, what's your name?"

"Fuck off, pookie bear. You're the one who started this. And none of your business."

The police left shortly afterwards, assured by Tristan that his "wife" would be protected and safe. And no, she didn't—*sniffle, sniffle*—see the gunman, but he did have a "big old gun," and if she thought of anything, anything at all, she would be sure to call them. As soon as the door closed behind them, she turned on him, the ungrateful wretch.

"So, you wanna tell me how I just happened to be in your mother's care a few days ago?"

CHAPTER SIX

"How did...I didn't..." Tristan took a deep breath and counted to ten. She was the biggest irritant he had ever met. And a slob. He reached over and started to button the flannel shirt she had on over her black t-shirt. Did she own anything else, he wondered, but black? Then he remembered those panties and bras. Those were definitely not black, but fire engine red and bright daffodil yellow. Oh, those were very nice. When she smacked his hands away, he huffed at her.

"I've been dressing myself for a long time, so back off." She sat down on the only chair in the room and began putting her shoes on.

She had tumbled from the bed right after asking about his mother and went limping badly into the bathroom, grabbing the emergency room bag with her clothes in it on the way. He had watched her walk away from him; the gown offered him a perfect view of the long line of her back. It was too bad that she remembered to hold the bottom of it together at the last minute. He wondered what color she'd put on today.

"Why would you wear such a garment and not wear it properly?" He had made the bed while she was dressing. Who made hospital beds before they left? he wondered, and decided he'd muss it before they left. Maybe. Okay, he knew that he wouldn't, but figured he should get points for at least thinking about it. Somehow, he didn't think the woman in the chair would give them to him.

"You have on a suit and tie in the middle of the night. Don't harp on me and my clothing, you nerd. You have enough issues of your own to deal with. What are you doing here anyway? And you never answered my question about your mom."

Her shoes tied, she leaned back in the chair. She looked weak and dizzy all of the sudden. He wanted to take her into his arms and hold her, but thought he might be able to keep more of his manly parts if he didn't.

"My mother was keeping an eye on you while I had other issues to attend to. I would appreciate it if you refrained from doing anything like that to her again. What's the matter with you, you look pale?" He felt guilty about the taste he had taken of her, but he wouldn't regret it. Her taste still lingered in his mouth and on his tongue.

The woman didn't answer him, but sat there for a couple more minutes before the nurse walked in. She looked surprised the see her up and about.

"Oh my, but you're up! I didn't…you were shot only hours ago. I'm sorry, I'm glad you're up." Nurse Jenkins was obviously flustered and Tristan hated making her feel that way. When he started to explain how she was a quick healer…the girl in the chair spoke up. Tristan really needed to know her name

"I would like you to get my papers to leave ready please. I'd like to go home with my…" She waved a hand in his general direction. "Whatever. Could you get them for me?"

The woman stood in front of the nurse and waited for her to look at her. When she did, she captured her eyes, the green of the girl's darkening to a deep forest color. The nurse immediately seemed to relax, to become unfocused.

"My papers for an immediate discharge, I need for you to bring them to me. And any paperwork that pertains to me must be destroyed after I leave today. You'll need to get them now, please."

"Yes, of course. You'll be leaving us today, right now. I'll just go and get your paperwork ready. And tomorrow morning, I'll make sure that they are shredded. If you'll just wait here, I'll be right back."

After Nurse Jenkins left the room, Tristan stared at the girl. She'd just enchanted that woman, and quite easily too. There was definitely more to her than humanly possible.

"What are you?" He was awed by her. Not only that, maybe just a tad frightened. She was more than he'd bargained for.

"A laboratory rat that went horribly, horribly wrong and should have been put out of everyone's misery. Now, if you'll excuse me, I have people to kill and money to make." She turned toward the door and slammed her nose into his chest. She immediately stepped back two paces. "What?"

"You are not going anywhere until I have some questions answered. Sit." He stepped toward her and pointed to the chair.

"Do you want to train me to piss on the newspaper too? I assure you, I'm completely house trained." She grinned then. "Well, maybe not completely. I do have a nasty habit of ripping hearts out of chests when I'm pissed."

"You don't frighten me." *Not overly much*, he thought. "Now sit down. I don't have all night, the sun will be up soon, and we have a long way to go before I'm satisfied you understand how I am to fit properly into your life from now on. There will be rules about you moving about the world on your own. That will stop without proper care on your part."

"Of course, your dickship. While I'm bowing and scraping, would you like for me to lick your boots as well? You can just..." She leaned in and sniffed his throat. Tristan felt his cock go from semi-hard, a perpetual state around her, to rock hard in a nanosecond. "You? Oh my God, you healed me? You gave me your blood, didn't you? Well shit, shit, and double shit! Do you know what you've done?"

She started advancing on him; he backed up. Her eyes had darkened again, that deep, deep green that he found he was beginning to love. Then stopped that thought before it could get him into trouble. More so than he was currently in.

"I was called to help and to save your life. And I did, so yes, I healed you. You would have been dead had I not.

But that does not negate the fact that things have changed. You must learn to—"

"You had no right! No right at all! Do you think that I want to live like this? Do you think that I do this job because it fulfills me? You insufferable prick. I...I should..."

Her growl startled him. It was deep and sexy, low, and purred along his skin like a caress. Tristan thought he was going to need a therapist when this was over. He'd gone off the deep...deeper end since meeting her.

She turned quickly, and he moved forward again to catch her, but it only made him a closer target. She came back around in a roundhouse punch that caught him square on his right jaw. Pain unlike he'd ever felt before reverberated through is entire body. His head exploded first from her fist connecting to his jaw, then when his head connected with the wall behind him. He dropped to the floor and slipped away.

When he came around a few minutes later—thank God for the regenerative powers of a vampire—he was still on the floor of her hospital room. She, of course, was nowhere in sight. He stood up slowly and ran his hand along his jaw, wincing at how tender it was. Then he felt for the knot on the back of his head and his fingers came away with a few drops of blood. Christ, that woman could deliver a punch! And shit! He was no closer to figuring out her name than he had been before.

He reached for her and found that she was still in the hospital, downstairs in the main area. Ah, billing. He grabbed his briefcase and went to find his lovely mate. He stepped into the elevator and pushed the button to go down. When the doors closed, he could only stare at the reflection that looked back at him in the stainless steel doors.

His clothing was disheveled, his tie askew. He saw a stain on his shirt and lifted the spot to his nose to inhale the small drop of her blood he'd spilled. But it was his face that startled him. The smile on his own face was so unfamiliar to him. He nearly looked behind him to see who could be standing that close. She had just knocked him for a loop, disobeyed him, and he was smiling. He had been too long without his solitude. She was affecting his mind, slowly driving him insane.

~~~

She was standing there crying when he came up behind her. When she saw him, she turned her back to him and wiped furiously at her face. When she turned back, she glared at him when he handed her his handkerchief. She laughed as she took it.

"What?" He didn't look amused. But then she thought he was always scowling at one thing or another when she was around.

"Only you would carry a real cloth handkerchief when there are, oh I don't know, perhaps fifty different brands of tissues on the market." Bailey blew her nose and tried to hand it back to him. Of course he didn't take it.

"They tend to be unsanitary and human diseases abound. We may not be able to catch anything from them, but we still don't have to be subject to their germs."

He hadn't referred to her as human, she noticed. He was correct in that, but for some reason, it bothered her. She was about to tell him to get lost again when she remember that he'd given her blood. She smiled when he flexed his jaw and rubbed it.

"Did you take mine? My blood, did you take mine too?"

"Yes. I…what's your name? Please tell me your name." He moved closer to her and she tried to back away. The woman behind the counter came from behind the stacks of filing cabinets just then or Bailey wasn't sure she would have moved back more.

"I'm sorry, Mrs. St. James, but I don't got no billing for you down here already. Do you thinking maybe it's been under a differ name?" Her English, while butchered, didn't hurt Bailey's ears as much as some people's version of what they thought was English might should like when they were faced with something they didn't know. But she understood her well enough.

"No, I'm sure it's just delayed. I'll be in tomorrow to pay for the billing." Bailey glanced at her name tag. "Shanna, right? Shall I ask for you then?"

"Yes, missus. That'll be fine. I be in at eight o'clock. Billing usually have the new ones down to us at that time. If you ask for me, I will help." Bailey smiled her thanks.

After the woman walked away, back to her cubbyhole, Bailey turned to Tristan. She had never really looked at him, and found herself mesmerized. He was a superb species of a man if maybe a little uptight; well, okay, he was a lot uptight. His hair was long, just curving up at his collar, and the color was a rich, shiny black. It was so thick, it begged to be tousled. She wanted to, too, to tousle him completely. He also had a deep widow's peak. His eyes were dark blue and she knew that they could be darker, because they deepened, getting redder when he was angry. She had yet to see him happy, thinking he hadn't been so in a long, long time. She didn't know if they lightened when he smiled, but wasn't willing to get too attached to find out. His jaw was hard and strong, the bruise she had given him already fading. He was taller than her by nearly a foot, and outweighed her by a good seventy-five pounds of pure male muscle.

But it was his voice; it was deep and soft at the same time. His accent, though slight, made her skin prickle with goose bumps, and when he whispered through her mind, well, she just wasn't going to go there. Suffice it to say, she needed a quick trip to the ladies room to cool her cheeks. Other parts of her body wanted relief too, but that so wasn't happening. He drove her so crazy one minute she wanted to hit him, then he'd get close to her and it was all she could do not to strip him down and taste him.

"I'm hungry. For food. And I have to tell you what will happen now that you've taken my blood. I...I'm not...it will make changes in you. You need to know what to expect. Then I want you to go away and leave me alone. We have nothing in common, other than you drive me as bat-shit as I do you. So do we have a deal?"

He looked at her for a few long tense seconds, then stepped up to her and pinned her to the counter that was just behind her with a hand on each side of her body. His pressed tightly up against hers.

"No." He leaned in slowly and brushed his lips across hers in a featherlike touch. Then again, slightly harder, more firmly, breathing her in. She flicked out her tongue to taste him on her mouth. When he groaned and ran his tongue across the seam of her lips she had just dampened, her entire body felt it. When she opened for him, he took her voraciously, devoured her, and consumed her. Bailey's hands tentatively touched his shoulders, moved lightly across them when he put his hands to her elbows and pushed them up to encircle him. He then pulled her to him, one arm around the small of her waist, the other tucked deeply under her neck.

The world ceased to move. Nothing else mattered but his mouth on hers, his body pressing against hers. And when he slid his leg between hers and pulled her harder against him, she moaned, deep from her toes. Her body was on fire for his.

"Excuse me! *Excuse me!* This is a hospital, not a brothel. I will have you know that we frown upon that sort of behavior here. You will need to take this elsewhere, preferable somewhere in private." The woman's voice cut through the haze of sexual fog like a knife.

Bailey jerked away from Tristan so fast she banged the counter and knocked a vase off. Had it not been for his fast move, it would have shattered on the floor. She moved to her left, getting as far from him as she could. What the fuck was wrong with her?

"I'm sorry, I…we didn't…I…he kissed…"

Bailey ran her fingers across her lips that were still warm, no, hot from his mouth being against them. He watched her so intently that she couldn't have made a coherent thought or decision if her life depended on it. He had literally rocked her world and was continuing to do so. He glanced at the woman behind them and answered for them both

"Thank you, I do apologize, but she was in a terrible accident today and I was just so happy to find her all right that I…well, you know how newlyweds are. We just can't get enough of each other at the best of times. Do forgive us, we'll be going now. Come, love, we should let this nice lady get back to work." He held out his hand. She knew that once she took it, things were never going to be the same again. Bailey closed her eyes and put her hand into his.

He took her hand and half-led, half-dragged her out of the building. He had her seated in a nice pub and a glass of water in front of her before she was able to respond.

"You…you kissed me."

"Yes, so glad that you noticed. You kissed me back as well. And I must say, you did a very nice job of it too. I'd very much like to do it again in the very near future." He had a tone. She didn't like it either.

"Don't be insufferable. Why? I don't understand why you'd even do something like that, especially to me. I mean, don't I…you know, the tissue thingy? Don't I have, I don't know, millions of germs on me too?"

"It was a chance I was willing to take. A lot." He moved closer to her on the bench. "I'd very much like to take another chance right now. You taste like ambrosia to me. Fresh oranges much like the blossoms on the tree in our front yard where I grew up."

When he moved over on the bench to kiss her again, she stopped him with a hand to his chest. This had to stop. They couldn't do this. At least she didn't think they could, but the closer he got to her, the less and less she was beginning to remember why.

"Now you stop right there. This is just as much a public place as the hospital, and I don't want you...you can't...you can't just go around kissing people willy-nilly like that. I don't think...you can't want to kiss me. I'm...I'm not right." She realized he had turned her into a ninny. Bailey hated ninnies.

"How are you not right, love? You certainly tasted all right to me, delicious as a matter of fact. But maybe I should have another taste, just to be sure."

This was the third time he had asked for a kiss. This time, she wasn't fast enough. He cupped her head with his hand, jerked her to him, and sealed his mouth over hers before she could protest.

His tongue dueled and danced with hers, sliding along it, and he sucked it into his mouth. He pulled a shadow around them. She was glad for that. She didn't want to be interrupted this time, not until she had her fill of him, of his mouth and taste. Bailey was afraid that this was only the beginning and it terrified her beyond reason.

"Your name, love, tell me your name." He whispered through her mind, low and urgent, soft and sexy. She couldn't have refused him even if she wanted to. And she most certainly didn't want to.

"Bailey, I'm...my name is Bailey Morrison. Please, you must stop, you can't...Oh God, yes!" He cupped her breast in his palm, brushed his thumb across her hard peak.

His moan moved through her, touched her in places she thought to be long dead, her heart for one. He pulled her closer, over him and onto his lap. Her legs instinctively straddled his thighs and she pressed her body, her heat, closer to his cock. His hands cupped her ass, cradling her to him as he showed her what he wanted, showed her how to ride him. He reached down between her thighs, and pressed his thumb against her clit through her jeans. Over and over she rode his fingers as he pressed his cock hard against her.

She was going to come and come hard. When he licked the pounding pulse at her throat, just as she was doing to him, he nearly sent her over the edge as he nipped at her. She needed him, wanted him. He sank his teeth into her the moment she did hers. Her fangs sank deep and into him and he came with her, exploded with an unexpected roar that tore out of her.

She forgot they were in yet another public place.

~~~

"We will never be able to step foot in that restaurant again. I hope you're happy. And I never got to eat. Food, I didn't get any food. I told you there was something you needed to know. I can't believe we did...shit, us...we?" She wouldn't look at him.

"Yes, love we did. And I'll feed you. Just tell me what you want to eat and I'll have the driver stop and we'll get it. You'll need to keep up your strength." He touched her, ran his fingers down her arm and up again. He loved the way she reacted to that, the slight shudder that raced through her body and into his.

"Don't you even care...of course you don't. Why should you? It's probably like some Tarzan thing, the equivalent to pounding on your chest, us being thrown, literally thrown, from a restaurant because we were...because we. Stop smiling, it is not funny. Sheesh, you're impossible." She looked out the window again. "Where are you taking us?"

"To my home. We can stay there and…talk."

His tone suggested something other than talking, and he did want everything from her. He was suddenly glad she was too fuzzy to realize what he'd done. Tristan wanted her beneath him as soon as they walked in the door. Now would make him just as happy, but he wanted a proper bed this time and he needed to be inside of her, deep and hard.

They had nearly had sex on the bench in a restaurant. He wondered what his brothers would think if they knew. They wouldn't believe him, he knew it. But every person in that restaurant did and had stared at them after they had come. They had both yelled, quite loudly as a matter of fact, yelled out their release. Tristan thought Bailey had it right. It was a Tarzan thing. He lifted his fist to his chest and pounded it twice just for the thrill of it.

"You have a home here too? Sure, why not? I guess if you live a million years you can own just about anything you want. And don't look at me like that, you arrogant ass." Tristan glared at her when she continued to call him names. "You have no idea what you've done."

"Oh, but I do. We have mated, bonded in the way of my kind, our kind. You are my true mate, Bailey, love. And we've taken care of the final part in a very public place and once we talk, because as much as I'd like to take you again right now, bury my cock deep into you, I realize there are things we need to discuss. But mark my words, as soon as the last word leaves my mouth, you are going to be flat on your back, naked, with me pounding another release from us both."

"I think…" Her cell phone chirped at that moment. She dug around in her pocket until she found it. Not even looking to see who it was, which he found curiously odd, she answered.

"I can't talk right now. And a printing job is out of the question for you right now…no…you told me…you said that it was clear…a clean print up. It wasn't." Her pauses were getting longer, the voice at the other end louder. He felt her pull a shield down the moment she answered, so that all he could hear was her end of the conversation and loud noises from the other. "Bonus aside…okay triple that and I'll think about it…shit…yes. Send the job to the main office…fuck off." She put the phone back into her pocket and he could feel her anger.

"Bailey, I suppose if I asked you what that was about you wouldn't tell me, would you?" She was silent for so long that he thought she wasn't going to answer. When she did, he wished that she hadn't.

"I'm a hired killer, Tristan, a hit man. I have killed seventy-three people in the past eleven years." She looked at him then. "So if you know anyone who has a lot of power, I suggest that you ask them to reverse this bond you say we have. And soon."

CHAPTER SEVEN

They didn't speak the rest of the ride to his home. When she had started to tell him more, he simply held up his hand to stop her. She slid away from him to the other side of the car and he let her, releasing her hand as well as his warmth. She should have figured it would happen. She had never told anyone what she did before because of this very reason. She reached out to the only other person in the world she trusted.

"Griff, I have a rush job coming in. It may arrive by this morning. I want you to contact me as soon as you get it. I will also need some cash. Can you manage that, please?"

"Yes, mistress, anything you wish. I am at your command, as always. How much do you need? And who am I sending it to?"

She frowned at his question. Who was she anymore? *"The name, I don't know yet. I may need to get something more very soon. Send the usual."*

"I understand." He hesitated for just a second and she waited for him to ask. But he didn't. She wasn't sure what

she would have said if he had asked her if she was all right. But what he did say didn't surprise her either. *"I will take care of the rest, all the identification as well. Also, mistress, there has been someone checking for you, under your name. It appears someone has found you."*

It was both of their fears that someone who had gotten away from Co-Tech would find them and begin the project again. They had destroyed everything in the building that night, but nothing was perfect. The people had gotten out, they had made sure of that. Also the prisoners, those that had wanted to leave. The rest, the ones who just couldn't stand to move among humans, had stayed behind when the building went up. She tried her best not to think about that.

She glanced over at Tristan. He worked fast, and she'd only told him her name about an hour ago. Since she had been with him since she had given him her name, she could only assume that he was contacting another of his kind by telepathy.

"How long do I have?" She asked him, knowing it didn't matter. The man sitting next to her not only had her real name, but he'd seen her as well.

"I have set up the usual blocks, so you will have no more than forty-eight hours. Less if they have good connections with money to spare."

"Count on both," she told him. *"All right, I'll need to know the particulars as soon as you get them. Thanks, buddy. Night, my friend."*

"Good night, mistress. Be careful."

The car pulled up in front of a castle, an honest to goodness castle, a few minutes later. Bailey had never been to a castle before, and didn't expect to spend too much time in this one.

She would give him what he needed to know and take off. She didn't know what they needed to do to complete their bond, or even if they had somehow already finished it, but she had a pretty good idea and had no intentions of letting that happen, not that she thought that he would want to anymore.

She'd heard of mated couples, of course. One couldn't be around other beings without some knowledge of their rituals. But she had never really studied the process and didn't really think it was all that big of a deal. He'd just have to find someone else to mate with. She was just too busy. Not that she held out any hope that after she talked to him he'd want it to happen anyway. There was an older woman standing in the doorway when they entered the estate.

"Maria, this is my mate, Bailey St. James. She will be staying with us," Tristan introduced. "Could you please show her to my room on the upper floors, and then she will require some food. Please, have Stanley see to that for her as well for me."

"Yes, my lord." She curtseyed to him and then turned to Bailey. "Mistress, would you please come with me? Will your bags be following soon, or shall I have someone pick them up for you?"

"No, nothing to follow." She left it at that.

The two of them went up the grand staircase to the second floor and was led into a massive suite complete with fireplace, sitting area, and bed, the biggest bed she had ever seen.

It had to have been at least half again as wide as even a king-sized bed and covered with the most beautiful array of colors that she'd ever seen. The deep, rich colors of the earth were a perfect match to the pieces in the room as well. Deep, dark cherry accented by lighter shades of yellows and greens. The drapes, closed now against the night sky, were heavy, hung on floor-to-ceiling frames, and looked as if they might have been made of velvet. In addition to the bed, there were two highboys and a long dresser. Along one wall was a massive shelf that was crowded with books, pieces of pottery, and objects of art. The hardwood floors had a scattering of rugs, all in the same colors of the spread. A pair of wingback chairs graced the fireplace that was lit with a cheery fire.

"Thank you, Maria. If you don't mind, I would like to rest awhile, please?" She wanted to think. And to plan.

"Oh yes, mistress. I'll let you know when the master…"

"Actually, I'm so sorry." She thought to rest, but it had been a long night and she might as well get it over with. "Could you take me to the master now? I have something I need to tell him."

"Of course. He would be in his…the study. If you'd like to come with me, I'll take you right to him." Maria had been surprised by Bailey changing her mind, but she recovered quickly.

Bailey had a moment to wonder how many other women he'd brought to his household under the guise of being his mate, then dismissed that thought. It was really none of her business and she was going to be out of his life soon enough anyway.

"I'd like to talk with you now if you please," she told him as soon as Maria left her in his study and closed the door.

No preamble, just straightforward, that was Bailey. A rip-the-Band-Aid-off-not-peel-it-slowly kind of girl. She almost grinned at that thought. Bailey rarely thought of herself as a girl much anymore, even less of person most days.

"Good." He nodded her to a chair. "I have a few things to say to you as well. You may start."

She tried not to bristle at that and his tone. One would never know they had nearly had sex in a public place not two hours ago.

"You asked me what I am. Well, I'm a lab project from a place that no longer exists. It was called Co-Tech Industries. We, a couple of friends and I, destroyed it about twenty years ago. There were three others that escaped with me twenty-two years ago next month."

"What does that have to do with—"

She cut him off. This was her story and she was going to tell it her way. "Tyler Dunn, now deceased, Griff Smith, and Charlie Smith, also deceased. Charlie died before we were off the property. He had been shot and had bled out before we could...well, that doesn't really concern you or what you want to know so I'll skip that part." She took a deep breath before continuing. "All that I'm going to share with you is how this may affect you, and it will. I was created in the lab, in a test tube actually. I'm the combination of several donors, all of them immortal races mixed together to try and create an elite super-race of beings that would be used for war. One of the donors was a vampire. That's why I could bite you. I also have the ability to do other things too. Whether it's magically, mentally, or physically, thanks to the DNA cocktail I was given, I'm pretty much a fuck up of all races."

"May I ask you a question?"

She wanted to tell him he just had, but thought he'd not appreciate her attempt at humor. She nodded.

"Do you know anything about the lab prior to it being destroyed? Who funded it? And who yet still lives?"

"No. We didn't care past getting out and surviving. There are others like me, marked like us, but...I have a mark, a tattooed bar code that was burned into my skin. They put it there when I was small. We all had one. But no, I don't know anything about the scientist."

"What things can you do? I've seen your fangs, but you said mixture. Of what?"

She was hurt by his dismissive tone that sounded like he didn't believe her. "I can shift into anything I need to so long as it has a heartbeat. I think that came from weres, a cougar and a wolf." Now, for the hard part. "We were considered a failure, and were set for termination a few days before we escaped. When you took my blood, you subjected yourself to all that I am, including everything I can do. You will be able to shift, if you couldn't already, your mental abilities will be exponentially stronger, also your strength. I can't heal myself, nor am I an immortal, but those will not affect you, as they are things that you had prior to drinking my blood."

"Did you have anything to do with Tyler's and Charlie's death?"

She turned away from him and looked out the window. Hurt ripped through her chest. "That would be the first thing you'd ask me, wouldn't it, Lord St. James?" She got up from the chair and paced around the room. "Indirectly, yes, I did. They were the only friends I had besides Griff and I convinced them we could make it on the outside world. The only people I ever trusted were these three and now two of them are dead. I will ever trust again except for Griff."

If he expected more, he would be sorely disappointed. Bailey felt him touch her mind, but she tossed him off. If he didn't want her then he had no right to trod on her painful memories.

"Bailey, love, I'm..."

She cut him off. "You will have your information about me soon. Yes, I'm well aware that you are having me investigated, Lord St. James. I have just as good of help as you do when I need information. I've had it slowed down a bit until we could...but your computer whiz will break through soon enough. I've seen his work before. He's quite good."

"Bailey, you have to understand—"

"I don't think so. Your information, it will be incomplete and most of it will be glossed over. But with what I've told you, you'll be able to guess the rest." She opened the window, leaned into it, and took a deep breath. "I want you to stay away from me, Lord St. James. If you come near me, or you send someone for me, I will kill them and then you. And have no doubt that I can and will. I'm a heartless bitch and can do what I want. There's a woman, the queen of magic. If you go to her, she'll help you get this...relationship you've found yourself in fixed. She doesn't care for me all that much anyway."

Bailey continued to look out the window. She wouldn't, no, she couldn't look at him. She had felt him touch her mind again, harder this time, trying to breach her hold, but she didn't allow him entrance. She didn't want him to see what he had done to her with his comment about Tyler. She needed to leave right now. She needed to get out.

She let go the first shimmer of magic then more power surged from her and around her. He watched her as her arms became covered in feathers, small white and brown feathers, as she held onto the sill. Then her hair changed, and with a snap, she was a falcon. A slightly larger than normal pedigree falcon with the greenest eyes known to man.

Bailey loved her bird of prey and how she made her feel in flight. Now, she was leaving. She hopped up onto the ledge of the window sill. He moved to her then, flashed to her and the window she had opened, but he was too late.

"Bailey, don't..." But it was too late. She was gone.

CHAPTER EIGHT

Tristan left the castle as soon as he could. Her scent was everywhere. He couldn't figure out how that was even possible as she had only been there for just under an hour. And in that same time frame, he had lost her. He wanted to scream out his frustration.

Aaron was in his study when he materialized in the main hall of the estate. He went in search of Duncan first, who directed him to the master.

"Master Tristan, if you don't mind my saying, you look rode hard and put away drippy."

Tristan could only stare at the man. He'd heard that Duncan had a new friend, Eon, the newest member of the local pack, who had been telling him idioms to use, slang, he had called it. Sometimes he messed them up a bit, but was cheerfully happy when someone helped him out. The half grin Duncan was sharing with him made Tristan think Duncan was having fun at his expense.

"It's wet, not drippy, rode hard and put away wet. And yes, Duncan, that's just how I feel as well." Tristan walked into the study like a man going to his own execution. He felt that way also.

Tristan sat down in one of the chairs across from the desk and looked down at his clothes. He was rumpled. Not only that, but he had another stain on his shirt. Damned woman was not only driving him crazy, but she was changing him as well. He reached down and tried to straighten his tie and looked up startled when Aaron cleared his throat. There was a smile there that Tristan thought he could gladly punch off the man's face.

"I..." Tristan stared off into space for a full three minutes before he continued. "I've found my mate. She's...she is...she has every right to be angry. I was stupid. And insensitive too. I asked her if she killed him. I'd like to think I knew her better than that. But I don't...feathers, they were beautiful, you know. So is she, beautiful, I mean. I...she can shift. Had I not seen it, I wouldn't have believed it, but she was covered in feather and then swish, she was flying away, taking my heart with her. I've come to realize I did too. Love her." He was taking a deep breath when Aaron interrupted him.

"Bailey, the girl you asked me to search for, I take it?"

"Yes." He wondered if that was what had pissed her off. "The information you sent was incorrect. She isn't human, nor did she kill those men. I know that...I knew it then. That's not to say she didn't kill anyone, but not those two. She's a hired gun, Aaron. A fucking hired gun."

Sara hadn't said much since she'd come in. Tristan liked the woman. She was very sweet, but could be a real bear when it came to her children. He wasn't sure she was really listening until she turned to Aaron and smiled. "I think you need to go and read a story to our wonderful children, love. They need you."

Aaron winked at her and kissed her nose then he looked over at Tristan. "Sara is my mate and I love her dearly, but she has connections that she shares with very few people. She is going to share them with you now, Tristan. It's a trust that I'm giving you that I give to very few. One of my mate being with you without me there to protect her. Do you understand what I'm telling you?"

Tristan did. It was a great honor to be left with a vampire's mate, a greater one when the vampire was a master. Tristan nodded.

"You have to understand something else," Sara told him after Aaron left the study. "What I'm about to tell you is something we don't share with anyone outside of this Kiss. I'm going to take you to the magical realm that is part of me, a part of all of us. And you will hear, see, and learn things that could very well rip apart the fabric of magic for everyone. Understand?"

"No. No, I don't. I don't understand anything right now. But I...I'm willing to keep an open mind. I'll try and keep an open mind." Tristan shook his head. "My life was so strict, so orderly, and then I met Bailey. You know, Mrs. MacManus, I don't think it will ever be that way again, and I find myself hoping it isn't."

"Please call me Sara, and honey, you ain't seen nothing yet." She reached over to the wall nearest the desk and tore a hole in the air. She just opened a portal and there it was, the castle that all magic was governed from.

Sara stepped through first and then Tristan. They were met by a company of men, the Royal Guard, she'd told him. They were there to protect her as the queen's cousin and to escort her and Tristan to the family room.

Tristan gaped at everything and everyone. When he looked up, there were perhaps six thousand tiny flies, but when he looked closer, he realized they were fairies. Tiny winged men and women going about their business, whatever that might be. Walking in front of him was a centaur and a smallish man and they were deep in conversation.

"He's a dwarf; his name is Paul. The centaur is Jakoal. They are in the Courts of Law-making area. And those aren't fairies, they're heather pixies." He looked at her, startled. "Yes I can read your mind. Over here there is nothing you can shield from me."

"Why am I here? I don't understand what this has to do with Bailey and me. You know something, don't you?" Tristan wasn't sure what he wanted to think about here, not if she could read his every thought.

She motioned for him to precede her into the large but cozy room. There were four people already in there waiting for them.

"This is James and Phillip and their spouses Savannah and Elizabeth. Phillip and Elizabeth are my grandparents. Mel is late, I see. Well, she is the Queen of Magic. Please have a seat."

Tristan remembered Bailey telling him to go to the queen of magic or something. He didn't get a chance to remember before a tray of drinks appeared before him.

"I understand that you are mated to the Printer. Oh my, that is amazing. What's she like?" Savannah said in awe as she reached for a glass of amber liquid and took a plate of cookies. "Like everyone else, we all assumed that the Printer was a male. To think all this time she was a female."

"The Printer? I don't understand. The hit man, that's my Bailey? Bailey is the Printer?" Tristan wished he could drink alcohol and a half glass of clear liquid appeared in his hand. He looked at the woman across from him.

"Go ahead, young man. Here you can eat food and drink something other than what you normally drink." Tristan set the glass down with a thud. Savannah grinned as she continued.

"Yes, Bailey, your mate, is a known assassin in our realm. We call on him…err her to help with our rogues. She was nicknamed the Printer because that is the front she uses, a print shop."

"When the information she needs is sent to her partner, it is sent to a print shop called Fine Printings, Inc. We use the girl quite a bit when we have a rogue that needs to be taken care of. I should have made the connection when Pete told us about the woman and Salvatore. She is good, very good," the man called James said. "I had heard that she is a chameleon. Is that true?"

Aaron had told Tristan about this man. James had a healthy fascination with all creatures and was working on a book to keep track of them. Pete was actually helping him, setting up a program on the computer to make access much easier and faster. Tristan felt like the rabbit that fell down a hole.

"No. Not a chameleon. She's a falcon…I guess one of her forms is a—how do you get a job like that? I mean, do you put an ad in the paper? How do people check your references when all your clients are dead? But I suppose that's the point, they're dead." Tristan had the overwhelming need to giggle.

He sat there for several seconds, thinking about her. Bailey really was a hired killer and these people, these beings, had hired her. She had been shot the other day, shot by the person she was hired to kill, or the police, but either way, they were directly involved in her getting hurt.

"She knew the consequences going in, Tristan. It's not like we didn't make things clear to her when we approached her." He stood when a woman of regal bearing walked in and sat down. "There were three of them when they started this, a were named Tyler Smith and a Cynogriffon called Griff. We have never met neither Bailey, nor Tyler for that matter. Griff is the only one we have dealt with as he is our only direct contact through the front. He's very protective of her."

"A Cynogriffon? I'm not sure...isn't that a mythical creature?" Tristan asked as he could almost feel the hole widening even further.

"Griff? No, he's as real as you or I. Griff is half eagle and half wolf, an extremely strong and a very intelligent creature. He is very loyal to the other two, or was. He never told us anything about them, not even when they were hurt or killed." Mel reached into the small basket that hadn't been there before, Tristan was sure of it. She pulled out an apple and another one appeared to take its place. He decided not to see it, simply not to see anything else or he would surely go insane. Elizabeth continued the tale.

"Tyler was murdered several months ago during an assignment he was conducting in the States. The only reason we heard about it was because we were asked to stop making payments into his account. It wasn't until his death certificate was sent to us that we discovered he had been killed. He had been shot twice in the head at close range. We tried to get in touch with the Printer, Bailey I suppose, but she had been working in another country. They all have been working for us for about fifteen years and her record is impeccable." A stack of folders appeared before him.

"You talk about her as if she is a Brownie troop leader, not some woman who murders other beings for money." He just stared at them, ignoring the stack beside him.

"I brought you those," Mel said quietly. "They're the last ten beings that she 'murdered,' as you called it, and why we had to call her in. The last one is Salvatore Madison. He was a black mage, dealt in the art of black magic. He was the man she killed the night you went to Paris to save Bailey, the guy that Pete told you about."

Tristan picked up the heavy folder and against his better judgment, opened it. As soon as the first picture appeared, he wished he could shut it again and found himself instead flipping through them. They were not only horrific but beyond what a person should know how to do to a body.

"As you can see, he likes his victims small and helpless, much like Pete Marshall's body type is," Mel pointed out. "He played with them, peeling their skin from them while they were alive. He used their terror and pain like you use blood. Their essences sustained him. We couldn't catch him. His magic in your world protected him and just when we would get close enough to bring him in for a trial, he would disappear."

Tristan looked at Sara from a picture of a young man. "That's Tyler, one of his many victims. I believe he was also one of his lovers. Someone, and now I can only assume it was your mate, found enough information for us to sanction his death. It took her a month, and he was setting up his next plaything when she took him out. Without her, another of our kind's mate would be dead, my friend Pete."

Tristan put his head in his hands and leaned forward. He was thinking he could really use that drink, and then he thought of drinking from her. The way she responded to him and him to her, and then he thought of the way he had hurt her, hadn't trusted her. Without raising his head, he told them all he knew.

"She is a creation—a test tube child. They were someone's idea of an elite race of beings to go to war. And no, she doesn't know who they were...but she may have an idea, but I don't know. I never... They considered her a failure because of something they hadn't counted on."

James was making notes, Tristan saw, when he looked up. When he paused, James looked over at him. "And the failure? What was it?" The room seemed to be waiting for his answer. He didn't like giving out that bit of information. It could be the life or death of her.

"She's a mortal. Her wounds heal like them, as does her busing. She told me she can be killed and that as my mate...as my mate, I will continue to be an immortal. She also told me to find you, Mel, and ask you to dissolve out bond."

"Is that what you want, Tristan? Not that I would, but is it?" Mel asked him.

"No," he answered her without hesitation. "No, I don't. She isn't a chameleon per se, but a mixture of immortal DNA. She can fly; I've seen her do that, and she claims...no, she said that she can shift into any living thing. I'm sorry to say that I didn't believe her when she told me. All I could focus on was that she was a hired gunman. Oh, and because I sipped from her, her powers are now mine. And before you ask, no, I've not tried to do anything. I didn't believe her. Not then." He looked up at Mel, his heart heavy. "I've lost her, haven't I?"

"No, not if I can help it. We need her, Tristan, but more importantly, she needs you. Without you two paired, you will die, and she will as well. The Fates have deemed this bond necessary. As for her mortality, she isn't. A mortal, I mean. When you bonded with her, she took your powers as well." Mel grinned as she tossed an apple at him. "We just hired her to work someone in the Netherlands. She will be back here in a few days. That doesn't leave us much time to plan."

CHAPTER NINE

Bailey was hidden in the shadow of a large building waiting for her assignment to walk out so that she could get this one over with. She never thought of them as people unless she was feeling low, which had been happening a lot since she had left Tristan's home two days ago. It seemed much longer sometimes. Anyway, her target was taking his own sweet time and she had too much time to think.

She was willing to admit that he had hurt her, but she wasn't willing to examine why it had hurt, or that he above all people, had been able to. She knew that she could be a bit harsh, maybe even slightly rude…okay, she was a bitch, she admitted, but she'd never asked for this. Bailey smiled when she felt a small touch of her mind and recognized the link. Griff, her friend, her only friend.

"Mistress, is this a bad time? I know that you are on assignment, but there is an issue you need to be made aware of before you return home."

"Never for you, my friend, never for you. What can I do for you?" She saw a group of men come out of the building, but none was her target.

"There has been someone in the print shop as recent as late last night. I do not sense anything taken, or any damage done to the equipment. There was a thorough search, though, but without malice or meanness of any kind. What would you like for me to do?"

Her first thought was Tristan, but she doubted he'd care enough after seeing her fly away and what he had gotten from the detective by now to care enough to search for her. Then she thought that closing it down and just quitting would be good, but she knew that she couldn't. She was still alive and breathing.

"Change the locks, contact the Realm, and let them know…Griff, did you feel anything, maybe any magic or 'others' there?" Griff was quiet. She knew that he was feeling the room, mentally touching each item to see what he could feel. He was probably angry with himself for not thinking of it too. She grinned bigger. It wasn't often she could outsmart him.

"Ah, yes, mistress, magic, or rather magic used to hide itself from us. You think the Realm is looking for something? You work for them, do you not?"

"We work for them and yes, I agree that it doesn't make any sense. Don't say anything for now. Let me think this through." Her target came out of the building and she had to move. *"My assignment is moving, so I have to go. Keep me updated and can you ward the doors around the outside and in? Give them a little something to remember us by next time, will you?"*

"Oh, of course, it would be my pleasure." His excitement was evident in his voice. *"Would you like them*

to remember with any certain part of their body, or may I decide?"

Bailey laughed out loud, startling a few people from their meal. *"You decide and have as much fun as you'd like. Later."*

"Goodbye and thank you."

She closed off their connection as she shifted.

Bailey was still grinning when she started across the street toward her target. He was fast, like a were fast, but she was a little faster while in flight. When he loped down an alley, she didn't follow, but stayed on the outer perimeter high on a balcony. Shifting back, she reached for a mental link to him and found he was with someone else. She followed the string to the other being he was talking to and listened in on their conversation.

"I don't think you understand," her target was saying. "I said this is the way it will go down, and that is the way it will happen. That stupid cow won't even know what happened, but she will when I'm done with her."

"We have to get rid of the other body before we take another. I mean, seriously, Josh, they start to smell fast when they're gutted like that and the neighbors might not like it. That's all I'm saying." The other man having a concern for his neighbors nearly made her laugh. They were both dumbasses.

"So, fucking get rid of it. Shit, do I gotta make all the decisions 'round here? It's not like we can use it anymore. Dead is dead, ain't it?" Josh snarled at his buddy as Bailey leaped to the ground as mist surrounded her.

"Oh, you have no idea how true that statement is," Bailey said as she walked out of the mist from behind them.

Bailey was behind the first guy before he knew she was there. Taking his chin in her hand and with a quick jerk, his neck was broken. That's when Josh decided to run, like that would stop her from finding him too. Decapitating the dead man with a quick blade to his throat, she shifted and took off after her target.

As a product of the lab, Bailey couldn't just keep her clothes on when she shifted, but anything in her hands or directly touching her skin stayed with her as well. If she'd had on her backpack, however, it would stay behind. It wasn't touching her so it wouldn't blend into her animal. Things in pockets, if they there wasn't too much metal, went with her as well. It made her armed and dangerous at a second's notice.

She caught up with him about a mile outside of the city limits. He had shifted as well and as a wolf, thought he could out run her. He'd been so wrong. Not only was her vision better than his as a falcon, she was much faster even with a back wind current.

When she landed outside the cave he had crawled into, she shifted back to human, pulled the darkness from the interior around her, and tightened down her shields. She didn't want him to hear her coming any more than she wanted him to get away. She moved toward the opening and went inside.

She was halfway in when she felt the hair on her neck tingle. Something was there too. Something dark and mean was close to her. Bailey had just pulled back when a huge claw that had come out of nowhere sliced through the air and missed her neck by a mere inch. She quickly realized it must have smelled the blood from the first kill on her clothes.

"So the Printer is a woman." A high-pitched voice said from beyond. "And a very pretty one at that, yes, yes, pretty indeed, she is. Oh, how I will enjoy the taste of you. Hummm, a tasty printer you will be."

She heard it lick its lips and smack them together. She reached out to it cautiously and found something she had never encountered before, a red dragon troll. They lived in caves or hill sides, carving out their homes or hovels with their sharp claws. The red troll was about medium height, but hugely fat and extremely lazy, waiting for his prey to come to them rather than hunt. Yet this one knew who she was. Even more curious was that he knew what she did. But she had a job to finish and no time to screw with him just now.

"What's the price, troll, to go about my business?"

That was another thing about them. They loved to make bargains. And they cheated at everything. And if one wasn't careful, a person could lose a great deal more than a bit of blood if the mood struck them.

"Ah, and she is smart. But you would need to be, would you not? Good, good, play you will with me? You wish to pass, my tasty morsel? Well, my price would be to answer three questions truthfully and correctly." The smell was nauseating; her stomach rolled a little at the tight confines of the cave that smelled of death, sweat, and old blood.

"No, one, and I'll only answer it correctly." She leaned to the right when she felt him moving toward her. "Two sides to every coin, troll. My truth could be your lie. Ask your one question."

He seemed to mull this over before he answered her. "You play unfair, but you are honest. I will ask one. You seek a being; you want a reward. You have its life, who will give you yours. What is he?"

She knew what he was asking her. She had no doubt of that. He was clever, this one, but still slightly stupid. She wanted to answer him quickly, but he'd be angry. She must make him work for it, or he wouldn't allow her passage without exacting another price.

"I seek no one but the were who came before me. I can track very well and he is here within your walls. Or have you made lunch of the fur ball? If that is so, then I need not play." She turned to go and smiled when he stopped her.

"No! I want my bargain." She heard what sounded like a foot stomping. "I will give you the other I have. I have treat for later. It will be a good trade too. You shall see, play the game, and you will have it for the answer. Deal, Printer?" He pleaded with her.

So the troll had eaten the wolf. Good, less work for her. But what else could he have that he had kept for a treat? When she reached beyond him, she felt nothing. Whatever he had captured, or had fallen into his hands, was deep into the belly of the cave. But if he had it to trade then maybe she could help the hapless soul who lay there.

"All right, troll you shall have your bargain. I have its life, who will give me mine. What is he? That which will give me mine is a vampire."

"But what of the rest of the riddle? You must answer it all. Play fair!" She heard him shift hard against the wall, and it sounded as though he stomped his foot again. Bailey wondered how old he was, and thought he couldn't be much older than maybe three hundred years old.

"We had a deal. You only asked one question and I was to answer it, and I did. If you wanted a riddle answered, then you should have said a riddle, troll, not a question. You got what you asked me. I told you what he is. Now, give over your treat, a deal is a deal." Her anger was evident in her tone.

He roared, making rocks tremble in his wake. Sparks rained across the stone close to where she was as his long, sharp claws angrily scraped down the stone walls in his fury. She nearly told him she'd play his way, but didn't like spoiled beings any more than she did spoiled humans.

"I will make no other deals with the Printer. No deals for the Printer, no more indeed. She does not play my games well. She does not cheat me, but she does not play fair."

"Troll, I am sorry, but I played fair." Bailey thought to reason with him anyway. "But I will give you another try. A question from me then. I will give you my first name for your trouble if you tell me one answer question. I will play fair, red troll." Why did she suddenly sound like Dr. Seuss?

"Deal! I will have my fun with you. You are a good being. Yes, good being indeed."

"I am the Printer, but how did you know? I gave you no clue, yet you knew when I first walked into your lair. Tell me how you figured it out."

"Ah, that is not so hard. Everyone knows of you. You have a smell of all of us. You are the maker of rights, righteous to the innocents of all the other beings. Yes, we all know of you and your were. You have the friendship of a Cynogriffon, do you not?" Glee filled his voice. "He is very powerful, yes, powerful in magic. We all love you, tasty or not. I do not wish your name, though it will make me envious of those who do not, but I will tell that you offered you to me. Yes, yes, I will."

Yep, they were both trying out for Dr. Seuss, or the little green guy from the Star Wars movies, whatever his name was. All they needed now was a light saber and things would be complete. She so needed a vacation.

"Thank you, troll. I am in your debt. You honor me with your kindness. If I may have your treat, please, I will bother you no more. But if I am in need of you, may I call upon your hospitality?"

"Yes, yes do. I will be honored to help the Printer. Yes, help you, I will. Thank you. You may have my tasty treat, hummm my treat." She heard him lumber away, taking most of the offensive smell with him.

What he tossed to her from the depths of his lair was a woman, a vampire to boot. The woman was in horrible shape, but alive. The troll was right in her being a treat for him. Eating a blood-sucker was a treat indeed for a troll. Bailey was suddenly glad that she'd made the deal with him. But she needed to get her help or she would die.

"Griff, I need a vampire and a donor at my location right now. Can you do that for me? I have a very weak female vamp and it has been about ten days since her last feed." She carried her out into the night and laid her on the cold ground.

"Yes, mistress, I will have someone there immediately."

It was ten minutes before the two men showed up. One was a master of this realm, the other a human servant. The human servant knelt before the woman and gave her his throat. Bailey looked away as the woman drank deeply, yet still didn't have the strength to get home on her own.

The master, Leighton Chalmers, a large Dutchman who had been around since the twelfth century, had also heard of the Printer. Sheesh, it was getting so a girl couldn't go anywhere without someone hearing of her.

"I am in your debt, my lady. Laverna is a very important female in our Kiss, as you are in yours, I'm sure. You shall have safe passage to the realms here in the Netherlands for your lifetimes, and my protection as well whenever you need it. I shall let the other beings know of your kindness to us." Leighton bowed low before her and kissed her hand in gratitude.

"I am very glad for your offer. I am, however, not a part of a Kiss. I live and work alone, sire. You have my gratitude, as well as the troll who found her. I would ask that he remain unharmed for as long as he lives. He could have kept her for his own rather than give her up."

Leighton looked at the mouth of the cave and shuddered. She didn't blame him. Trolls smelled bad and their eating habits were horrendous. He told her he would honor her request, as would all the other beings.

"I thank you. Now, I'm sorry, but I must go. I have to get back to another...I'm on an assignment." She shifted into her falcon and left him standing on the hillside. He looked at her oddly as she flew away, but she was too busy to think about what it might mean.

She flew back to the alley and gathered up what she could from the first man's scent to find the woman that they had been discussing. After throwing the piece of shit into the dumpster, she shifted to wolf and followed his scent back to the lair he had shared with the target.

The woman's body, another vampire, had been tortured beyond any hope of her being brought back, Bailey was saddened to see. She reached for the master again and told him of the grim discovery and where to find the body. He said he would make sure that things were cleaned up before the police were notified by a nosey neighbor, and he thanked her again.

Bailey took the next flight to the United States. She was in serious need of down time. Her body ached and she was tired beyond what she had been for some time. She told Griff to not take any more assignments for a few days. He agreed that she needed to rest as well.

She decided to take a long, hot bath when she got back to her house. She pulled her hair up in a sloppy knot on top of her head as she stepped into the warm water. While lying there, she thought of the pool she had seen at Tristan's home and how lovely it would be to sink down into its depths right about now.

Then her thoughts turned to his body and the way it felt pressed against hers, his mouth moving over her throat, down along her pulse. The way his blood had tasted to her, the richness of it, powerful and dark. She wondered how his mouth would feel on her skin, how it would feel to have him inside of her. Suddenly realizing where her thoughts were taking her, she jumped out of the tub and quickly dressed in her favorite jammies.

CHAPTER TEN

She was in her kitchen stirring the cocoa in the warmed milk when Tristan entered her house. He could smell her, the fragrance she had used in her bath, the lotion on her skin. Tristan could even smell her arousal, hot and spicy.

Tristan slipped up behind her and wrapped his hand around her waist with the other around her mouth so she wouldn't scream. Startled, her hand went to the weapon that wasn't there.

"Don't, Bailey, it's me, Tristan." His cock hardened when he pulled her to him.

He ran his hand up and down and around her waist and settled it over her belly, pressing her back into him. His mouth was moving slowly down her neck, nipping as it went. Her body, already relaxed from her bath, softened more as he touched her. When he felt her lean back into him, she pulled away and moved to the other side of the kitchen. Tristan reached over and turned off the burner under the milk.

"I'm sorry. I'm sorry about everything." He looked down at her pants, a pair of loose-fitting flannel lounge pants that tied at the waist, her bare feet peeking out from under the legs of them. The design nearly made him laugh, for they were a contradiction with their wearer. They were daisies and bunnies on a bright pink background. The top, a bright pink sleeveless t-shirt with a dead bunny on the front was more to her temperament. The shirt was tight, and her breasts were bare beneath it. As he stared at them, they swelled and tightened, and her nipples puckered and pushed hard against the material. His breath caught and his heart slammed against his chest.

When he looked at her face finally, he saw his own need and wants staring back at him. "Come to me, Bailey. Now. Come to me."

She didn't hesitate but launched herself into his arms, wrapping her body around his, legs at his hips and arms around his neck. He caught her to him and turned to press her against the closest hard surface he could find, which happened to be the refrigerator as he took her mouth in a searing kiss.

The cool, hard surface of the fridge at her back was in direct contrast to the hard heat of his body pressed to hers. He could feel that when he touched her. When he cupped her flannel-covered ass and pulled her heat closer to him, Bailey threw back her head and moaned loudly, giving him full access to her throat.

"I want you, Bailey, right now. I need to be inside of you."

He didn't wait for a reply but began working the material down her bottom so he could stroke the warm flesh it covered. Sitting her on the counter and stepping back, he yanked the pants from her and tossed them behind him just as he stepped between her legs. Reaching down, he pulled her shirt free of her body as well. Before it touched the table where he had tossed it, he had her nipple deep inside of his mouth, suckling it hard, his hands cupping her ass once again.

She bowed into him, pressing her breast deeper into him, and tightened her legs around his hips. The thong she had on was no match for their need for each other because, suddenly, they were just two scraps of lacy silk on the floor beside the bunny PJs. His shirt and tie went next and suffered the same treatment as her underwear, but her hands were touching his skin, his bare, hot skin and neither cared about the clothing anymore.

"Tristan, please, upstairs. The bed is upstairs." She whispered in his ear, and bit his lobe before moving closer to his neck and the muscles there.

"Never make it. Now, baby, I need you now." He stepped back again and his knees nearly buckled at the naked woman before him.

Her full breasts were shifting up and down because she was panting so hard, her nipples red and swollen from his mouth. Her pussy was soaked, her juices shining on the curls that just covered the nether lips he so desperately wanted to fuck and taste at the same time. "Christ, I want you."

He pushed her back against the cabinets and pulled her hips closer to the edge. He ran his finger along her heat from the bottom to the clit that was just visible beneath the curls. He teased her with a flick of his finger before pushing into her core.

Bailey nearly came off the counter, her hiss of approval driving him to deepen his assault. He watched her as he fucked her with his finger, soon adding a second then a third into her. She rode him, undulated her hips with each in and out movement of his fingers. Leaning in, he took her breast into his mouth again, scraping his fangs across the nipple, drawing a tiny bead of blood to the tip. He drank greedily from the hard peak.

With is free hand, he pulled the snap off his dress pants and jerked the zipper down. His thick, hard cock immediately filled his hand, a tiny pearl of cum oozing from the tip as he fisted it up and down in time with the movements of his fingers inside of her.

When he was close, feeling the tingle of impending climax running up his spine and straight to his balls, he pulled his fingers from her. Her moan ripped through him, nearly making his come all over her.

"I'm large, baby, I'm sorry, but it's going to hurt you. If you want me to, we'll...Christ, I can't believe I'm saying this, but we'll stop. We will, Bailey; do you want me to stop?"

"I've never...I mean, I don't know. Take me; please Tristan, I want you inside of me now."

Putting action to words, she tightened her legs around him once again and surged forward just as he entered her, breaking through her hymen with a hard push. She screamed with the pain as he took her virginity.

Tristan stopped, his body frozen inside of hers. He could feel her body adjusting to his, pulling and wrapping tightly around him. He wanted to move deeper, to empty himself in her, but he also knew that he'd hurt her more if he tried to move just now.

He kissed her gently on the mouth, kissed away her tears as they fell along her cheeks. All the while he was touching her, murmuring things to her, soothing her, holding her as he would a small child who had a hurt. His mind was frozen. He could no more tell himself what he'd said to her than the day of the week.

"Oh baby, I'm so sorry. I didn't…well, I did mean to, I just…as soon as you are ready, I'll pulled away, honey. Then a bath. I'll run you a tub full of hot water…Oh God, Bailey, don't move like that…oh yes, no, don't…Bailey, please."

She started moving, to move away, he was sure, but as soon as the friction of his cock moved against her clit, she moaned and he didn't think it was from pain. He held still, waiting for her to make the next move. She tentatively moved forward against him. He too moved, drawing a deep moan from her. His movements were slow, measured. He didn't want to hurt her, but he could feel her need building back up with every stoke of his cock.

"Oh, my God, Tristan, please. Oh please, don't stop." He knew he wouldn't be able to now, not with her legs tight around him and her pussy walls milking him.

Cupping her ass, he picked her up and holding her tight against him, he pressed her against the fridge again, using it for leverage. Their rhythm grew frantic, their moans deeper, more demanding. When he felt her tongue trace the vein down his neck, he knew he was lost. He began to ride her harder as he searched for the vein in her throat. Licking her rapidly beating pulse, he knew his own was pounding as hard as hers. He bit her then and drew a deep pull of her into him, his own blood pouring into her mouth, as she had bitten him too. Their mutual climaxes roared through them. Tristan didn't stop. His movement slowed as he held her closer to him and when she came again, sobbing his name over and over, he came hard, pouring himself deep into her.

Tristan leaned his head against the cool refrigerator, and tried to calm his pounding heart. He was panting hard as hell, his lungs burning. He held Bailey to him, his cock still semi-hard inside of her. He straightened enough to look at her. The sated look on her face took his breath away.

"Are you all right, love?" When she didn't answer right away, Tristan turned and sat her on the counter again. "Bailey?"

"I'm fine. No, I'm not fine. I'm amazed, overwhelmed, relaxed, happy, wowed. I don't know if I'm making any sense." She snuggled her face closer to his neck, licking the droplets of blood she had missed. She looked up at him when he growled at her.

"You keep that up and we will never leave this kitchen. I think you should have that bath. You're going to be sore, if you aren't already." He didn't put her down, but carried her still wrapped around him up to where she had pointed out her bedroom. The taps were on and the tub filling before they had gotten to the stairs.

As they were both naked, he stepped into the tub and settled them both into the water. Turning her around so that her back was against his chest, he began washing her with the large sea sponge that was sitting along the edge. There were candles all along the wall of the enclosure on little shelves. With a thought, he lit them for her, their scent wafting around the room. He ran the sponge up and down her arm as he held her, not really wanting to wash her so much as to touch her.

"How do I shift? I know you can do it, but I haven't been able to figure it out." He had tried twice just yesterday and had given himself his first headache. Not an experience he wanted to repeat.

"What did you want to become? I love the falcon, but I think you'd be too big for one." She shifted in the water enough so that his cock sprang to attention again. "You concentrate on the being, everything about him. His feathers, his beak, wings, all of it until you can see him as clearly as if he were standing right in front of you. Are you doing it?" She turned in his arms and straddled his lap, her thighs squeezing his.

"Well, I was until you did that. Let's see, his feathers...they must be as soft as your breasts." He touched gently them, lifting them just above the water's edge, and took a nipple into his mouth. "Hummm, they couldn't be this soft, nothing would be."

"Tristan, please, your aren't concen...concentrating very...oh yes, please." He suckled hard, teasing her with his teeth. Her body moved closer to him; her thighs gripped him more tightly.

"His beak, you said .I can't do this with a beak." He brushed his lips across her lips and tugged on her nipple at the same time with his finger and thumb. He moved her around and sat her onto the tub's deep rim, her back to the wall. Opening her legs wider, he moved between them.

"Tristan, what…please, I'm trying to show you something here, something…you said that you…I, you…what were we talking about?"

He grinned at her. Having her flustered was probably something no one had ever witnessed before. He liked it.

"I'm going to taste you, Bailey. I'm going to go down on you and lick you until you come in my mouth."

"Oh my." He could see the blush starting at her breasts, those lovely breasts, and move up to her cheeks. She was simply the most beautiful creature he'd ever seen.

He moved down to her pussy, lifted her thighs, and placed them on his shoulders. His first taste of her, a short swipe of his tongue against her heat, nearly made him roll his eyes to the back of his head. Mine! Mine, was all he could think. Using his fingers, he widened her nether lips and began exploring her with his tongue.

He began to fuck her in deep licks, bringing as much of her thick cream and his cum in his mouth as he could, loving the taste the smell of their combined juices. He slowly inserted his long finger into her, digging and reaching for the sweet spot just inside of her as he suckled at her clit. The soft noises she made encouraged him to moved deeper, take more of her, and to fuck her quicker.

When Bailey stopped breathing, her body winding tighter and tighter with every touch of his tongue, he knew she was very close. When another finger joined his tongue, she lifted her hips up and tilted herself for him to push deeper, take more of her, and taste her.

"I'm going to come, Tristan. Oh my God, yes, I'm going to come." She threw back her head and screamed, the sound bouncing off the walls of the little room and coming back to them.

Still, he ate her, lapping up her juices as fast as they emptied from her heat. When her tremors were just starting to slow, he lifted her, turned her around so that she leaned over the edge of the tub, her ass up and open, and took her from behind. Holding onto her hips, he began slamming his cock deep into her, riding her hard, bringing her to peak twice more. As he felt his own climax building, he leaned forward, pulled her up to her knees, and cupped her breasts in his hands. With a deep growl, he bit her neck deep hard, swallowing some and letting the rest of her blood run down her breast and into the water spilling out of the tub beneath them as he spilled his seed deep within her heat.

Tristan woke to an empty bed. The pillows were cool, as were the sheets. She had been gone for some time, he surmised. He closed his eyes, felt through the apartment and found that she wasn't there. He got up, as it was nearly dark, and looked in vain for a note.

He reached harder, further for her and found that she was indeed far, all the way in another realm. He'd never been able to reach there before and could only assume that it was in part because of his visit there several days ago. He swept gently into her mind, not even sure it would work.

"Love? You left me in a cold bed. I had such plans for us the rest of the night."

"I'm...I wasn't aware...I won't be back there for several days, maybe even as much as a couple of weeks." He could hear the surprise in her voice.

"I won't be able to go that long without you, without your taste. Let me come to you. I can be there soon." Overwhelming need enveloped him. He had never wanted to touch someone so badly as he did her right now.

"No. I...you can't. Can't come here, I mean. I'm...shit, Tristan, I'm working. What do you mean you won't be able to go that long? The sex was great, fantastic as a matter of fact, but I'm sure there are hundreds of women, and even some men that would kill to be with you. I can't have been that good." He could hear her insecurity in her tone. He tried to ignore the reference to other women, but he wanted her with him.

"I don't want anyone else, and as of last night, and the fact that we are truly bonded, I can no longer feed from anyone else, and I wouldn't even want to. Bailey, we are going to have to talk about this job of yours. I don't want you working like this anymore. It's dangerous and you could get yourself hurt or killed. I won't have it."

He knew as soon as he said it that it had been a mistake. Tristan knew better than to make demands of her. She was not only smart and stubborn, but she was also more capable of taking care of herself than he was. He wouldn't tell her that, but it was the truth.

"Look, bucko, you will have to understand something right now. I do what I want, when I want, and you will not dictate to me. No one does, understand me? I'm busy right now, and you will hear from me when I'm fucking good and ready." She slammed her mind shut to him.

He felt it, felt the tight rein she held around her so that he couldn't reach her any longer. Well, fuck, he'd screwed that up royally.

CHAPTER ELEVEN

She followed her target through the building and then out into the courtyard of a large mansion. Try as she might, she couldn't get the night before and then the conversation with Tristan out of her head. She didn't need this right now.

The being she was tagging was a fae. They were the trickiest of all the targets she had to contend with. Fae didn't play by anyone's rules except theirs, thus the reason she'd been called in. She was to detain and bring in for questioning and if that didn't work, then termination.

When he moved to an outer building, she moved in to capture him. He was close enough that she could smell him then. He was not only fae, but had some pixie in him, the sweet, clouding odor of flowers permeating the air. Just as he moved toward the street, she slipped the blade up and around him and slit his throat. He wouldn't die, not here, but it would be enough of a wound to slow him down until she could get him to the castle dungeon. She picked him up and threw him over her shoulder just as he was beginning to stir again, the wound having healed that fast.

"Where are you taking me? I'm of royal blood, female. You can't treat me like a commoner. Put me down you, you smelly vamp. I demand you bring me before your queen."

Bailey didn't recognize the queen, or anyone else in the realm. It made for a better working relationship for everyone if she kept a neutral stance. But this idiot didn't seem to realize that the queen knew of his…misdeeds.

"She's your queen, not mine, and that's where we're headed. Well, you are. I'm just dropping you off where they told me to put you. Now, shut up. I have a headache and you're not helping it." She smacked him hard against the wall and when he fell off her shoulder, she simply picked him up and threw him across her again. It was going to be a really long day.

"The queen wishes to see you." Bailey had just dropped off her target in the cell when a troop of eight Court Guard showed up. She eyed them warily.

"I have things to do, and no time for socializing, but tell her I said thanks." She moved toward them and stopped when they spread out, weapons at the ready. Not quite drawn out of their scabbards, but just enough that she knew they meant business.

"The queen wishes to see you now." This time, it sounded more like a demand than a request. Their hands pulling out the swords at their sides indicated that it was just that, and they didn't think she should be declining the invite.

"Eight against one is not really in my favor, so you may be able to subdue me, but that's about all. I don't want to have to hurt you, any of you, but if you pursue this, I will. Just tell your queen that I'm busy, and we'll all be a bit healthier tomorrow." She took a stance as well. Her weapon of choice was her body, it being just as lethal as their swords.

"Come with us, and we will allow you walk on your own two feet. If not, then you will be carried. Decide." The front man smirked at her. She didn't care for that. Nor his attitude. Well fuck them. She was having a shitty day and they had the bad misfortune to get the end of it.

She shifted into a dragon. A very large, fire-breathing, winged dragon. The men as a whole stepped back several paces. When she extended her wings, she was nearly thirty feet wide and her impressive ten foot height made her something to reckon with. Smirk now, she thought. Bailey stepped two steps forward then back one and shifted back to herself.

"I've decided that you will let me pass or I'll eat you for dinner. Now move." She stepped toward them and all but one stepped back. He hadn't been doing the talking, so she assumed the leader was somewhere in the back of their merry band.

"The queen only wishes a word, mistress. She said to tell you that you are all impressive and all, but she'd only like a word." She had to give him points for being persistent.

"Again, I'm busy. Tell her to call and make an appointment if she has a job for me to do. I do not socialize." She walked passed him and down the large entrance hall to the keep. She was nearly to the doors when a large dragon, a real one this time, stepped in front of her.

"I don't make appointments with my subjects. And you will do well to remember that next time I send for you. Hello, Bailey." Bailey closed her eyes and counted to ten before turning.

"Your grace. Since you hold the entire deck of cards, what do you want? I really don't have time for this. I have a lot of things to do and time is running short. The contract was for three beings and I've only delivered the one. I have a scant ten days to recover and retrieve for you." She turned slowly and took in the room and where all the queen's players were.

"Would you mind coming with me? Standing out in the open to talk to you is not what I had in mind when I asked you to see me." She fanned her hand in the direction she wanted her to go.

"*Asked* me to see you? Yeah, right, and here is just fine. I like the openness of this room. Again, your grace, what do you want?" Bailey settled her hands on her hips, her body loose and ready.

"Bailey, has anyone ever told you what a stubborn pain in the ass you can be? I want you to come with me into the salon. We have things to discuss and I don't want the entire castle to hear. Come with me now. Please?" All she needed to do was stamp her foot, thought Bailey, and the tantrum would be complete.

The first two guards fell from the second floor balcony and landed on the floor ten feet from the queen. The next four dropped where they were standing. The six that had bows and arrows pointed at Bailey froze, unable to move even their eyes. The other ten men, all with swords out of the scabbards, dropped like a set of dominos all in a line, falling upon each other, their weapons forgotten. With a sudden flash of light, the dragon in the doorway disappeared. In less than five seconds, the entire troop was disabled and the queen was held at knife point and at Bailey's mercy.

"I have things to do. I do not socialize. I don't want to talk with you. And I do not like to have people pointing sharp objects at me; it puts me in a bad mood. Do I make myself understood now, your grace?" She whispered each word directly into Mel's ear, enunciating clearly.

"You'll pay for this, Printer. And pay dearly. No one touches the queen without permission." Mel had not counted on Bailey's magic working in her realm, apparently. "When I gave you free rein so that you could work unfettered in my realm, it wasn't so that you could attack me."

"Then by all means, kill me. I will happily go to the guillotine, just say the word. I tire of this life anyway." She tightened her grip on the queen for a scant second, and then pushed her away from her. "Don't threaten me with my demise, your grace, I've stared death in the face more times than you can even imagine."

Bailey delivered the other two beings over the next eight days. The second one had cut her shoulder badly and it had taken her a day to deal with the pain and be able to move again. The third man, another fae, decided that fighting her was much preferable to the cell he was destined for. The severe burn to her back from a blast of heat caused her to move much slower and he was able to slice her leg open with a claw as well. Taking his head was a pleasure after that.

"Would you like for someone to treat those for you? We have a healer on staff for us and there is also any number of witches here that could give you a potion to ward against infection."

The guard at the gates of the cells had been very standoffish since she'd tried to eat them. She normally didn't care, but just lately she had become very concerned when she came to the queen's realm. This one had spoken to her before. She could feel his fear of her, but it didn't stop him from being polite.

"No thanks. I just want to leave this place." She turned to go and there stood an entire company of men.

"My lady. The queen asks that you please join her in the salon if it is convenient for you. She said that she only wishes a word with you."

The man looked nervous, and Bailey remembered him from last week. He had been one of the guards holding an arrow at her. Bailey also noticed that none of them were touching their weapons. She made sure she didn't make any sudden moves toward them when she took a step in their direction.

"All right. But tell her that I'd rather be out of doors, please. I stink and I don't want to smell up her pretty room." Bailey hadn't had a proper bath for nine days. She'd swam in the lake near the mountains in this realm, the water cool and clear, but as there was no soap or shampoo, she was feeling a little dicey. She was sure she smelled that way too.

She followed the men out onto a large open area that surrounded a beautiful in-ground pool. Trees, bushes, and pretty flowers were scattered about, as were several lounge chairs and tables and chair sets with umbrellas. Sitting at one of the tables was Tristan, and he wasn't alone. There were two other men with him.

"Bailey. I've missed you. I was wondering if I might have a private word with you before the queen arrives." Tristan stood up and took her hand as soon as she was within several feet of his table. He started pulling her along behind him at a fast clip into the wooded area behind them.

"Where are you tak—" She was suddenly pressed against a wall and her mouth was being devoured by his. She tried talking around his mouth.

"Shut up, just shut up and kiss me." He had pulled away long to make that demand, then went back to kissing her.

She felt his cock, hard against her belly, and melted against him. Apparently, she had missed him too, she thought with a giggle. She pulled his shirt free of his pants and raked her nails hard across his warm skin, drawing a trace of blood for her efforts. She was rewarded with a deep moan from Tristan that she could almost taste and a shudder of his body.

"Please, I want you. Please, Tristan, inside of me now." She was already working at his belt. Did the man have to wear so many fucking clothes? When his snap was undone, she reached her hand into his trousers and cupped his shaft in her palm. This time, she moaned.

"Christ, I only wanted to...Bailey, stop, I have to...yes, harder, harder. Bailey, please." She had her hand wrapped tightly around him now and was stroking him hard up and down, faster and faster.

He jerked at her zipper and yanked her pants and panties off her in one move; he pushed her shirt up over her breast and ripped the bra in half. Her shoes had disappeared sometime just before she touched him. The tie wasn't cooperating so she just moved it away, ripped his buttons from his shirt, took his hard nipple into her mouth, and bit him while tugging it down his arms.

"Turn around. I'm going to fuck you here. Turn around." When she didn't move fast enough, he tossed her around and against the wall, still partially dressed, slamming his body against hers.

"Please. Please now." She pushed her body back against him until his hard cock was cradled in the crack of her ass. She started riding him this way, moving up and down him until he growled at her.

"Bend over, Bailey. Bend over and grab your knees. I want you too badly to wait. I'm going to fuck you."

She bent over and before she could get a grip on her legs, he was slamming into her heat. His size tore into her, making her cry out in pain, but he didn't stop and she didn't want him to. Gripping her hips, he slammed into her hard. Soon she was backing into him with each slam of his cock into her. She reached between her legs and touched his balls, which were tight against him, and squeezed him, rolled him gently in her hand. He stood her up then and pressed her against the wall again, his cock still deep within her. She felt his teeth scrape along her shoulder through her shirt, when suddenly he ripped a tear in it and he had his mouth on her skin. His hand moved between her legs, widening them for his touch.

"Please..." When he pressed his thumb against her clit, he sank his fangs deep into her neck where her shoulder met. She came apart, crying out her release, and Bailey barely heard his cry of completion, her own cries reverberating along the wall.

He continued to feed, taking her into his body and moving against her. His cock was still semi-hard and inside of her, making her need him again. She sent him that need and felt his cock harden immediately. Sealing the tiny wound at her neck, he turned her around and kissed her. Bailey could taste her blood on his tongue, mixing them together in a way that had her pussy weeping again.

He must have sensed her need because he dropped before her and buried his face between her legs, licking and sipping from her core. Lifting one of her legs, he rested it on his shoulder as he moved further between her thighs, suckling and nipping at her. Knowing that he had to taste his cum as well as her own had her close to coming yet again. When he pulled her ass cheeks apart and began rubbing the small rosebud of her ass, using their combined cum as a lubricant, she growled deep in her throat.

"I'm going to fuck you here soon, Bailey. I'm going to claim this tight hole like I did your pussy. My cock is going to come deep in you here. You're so tight, so fucking tight." When he slid his finger into her, she moaned at the pain and the pleasure his intrusion had created.

"Please." Mindless with need, she began moving against his mouth harder now. She couldn't think beyond what his fingers were doing to her. When he slid a second finger in with the first, stretching her tight hole, and suckled her clit into his mouth and bit her, she came, screaming this time, long and loud. While her body was still trembling with release, he stood and entered her again, her wet heat making the slide in easy and swift. Lifting her and locking her ankles behind him, he began moving hard against her again. Tilting his head for her, exposing his throat, she bit him, drawing deep on his vein, her body exploding again as he released his seed into her.

CHAPTER TWELVE

"Are you all right?" It had taken Tristan a few minutes to learn to breathe and then to get his heart moving at a normal pace. He was still pressed inside of her with her against the wall. He knew that she was alive. He could hear her heart pounding along with his.

"Yes. I...you made me come four times. It was incredible!"

"We could try for five, but I know that it'd kill me." He heard her giggle. He pulled back a little and looked down at her face. Reaching up, he gently traced a bead of sweat trickling down her brow. "I never meant to hurt you, but I find that once I'm near you, I can't seem to get enough of you."

"I usually have the opposite effect on people."

A laugh burst from his lips, something that had only happened when she was around. "I wanted to bring you over here to talk to you, to feed maybe. I...making love to you wasn't what I had in mind."

"I didn't start this, Tristan, you did." She pulled away from him and reached down for what was left of her clothes. Her bra was trash, as were her panties. She sat down and began pulling on her pants.

"I didn't mean it like that. I just meant…what the hell happened to your leg?" He was pulling her pant leg back down to get a closer look at the wound. It was about ten inches long and had cut deep into the muscle along the outside of her leg from just above the knee to the ankle. He was surprised he hadn't seen it when he ripped her pants off, but he had been a little distracted at the time. It looked as if someone had tried to stitch it closed, but they were now pulled loose and the gash open again.

"It's nothing. Leave it alone. I'll just have to close it again—" He opened it up with his fingers. "Ouch! Damn it, be careful."

When she had jerked away from his touch to her back, he flipped her over onto her stomach to look at the burn there. It was deep and angry-looking, spreading from just under her shoulder to above her left hip and about a foot across at the widest point. The blisters had burst, more than likely from being rubbed against the wall. Looking up where he had taken her, he saw blood smears.

"Why the fuck didn't you say something? Christ, I'm not an animal. I would have waited." His fangs had dropped and his eyes turned in his anger. Not at her, though she deserved it, he thought, but at himself.

He started to pick her up and she fought him, slapping and kicking at him until he had to back away or hurt her more. He looked down at her and her tear-streaked face.

"Stay away from me, you stupid jerk. You got your food and fuck, just like you wanted, now stay away. If you want another one sometime, contact Griff. He'll know how to get in touch with me." Moaning, she pulled her pants up, grabbed her tattered shirt, shifted into her falcon, and flew away.

He was still sitting there on the ground, half-dressed, looking toward where she had flown when Aaron found him.

"Tristan?" Aaron began.

"She's hurt, again. How do I keep her safe if she is in constant danger? And how do I stay with her when she only needs to shift into something and fly away from me?" He looked back at the master and realized that he was laughing. "I don't find any of this the least bit funny. What is it?"

"You. And her, but mostly you. Look at you, all rumpled and messed up. There are no buttons on that shirt and your tie is hanging around your neck backwards, and I believe your zipper and button to your pants are over there in the tulips. What I wouldn't give for a camera right now. *Oh wait!* My cell phone!" He began digging it out of his pants pocket with full intentions of taking a picture.

Tristan growled and leapt at the man, knocking the phone free of his hand and Aaron to the ground. The fight might have been a little more evenly matched, but Aaron couldn't seem to stop laughing long enough to take it serious, so he ended up with a bruised jaw and a busted lip. Tristan had a black eye and a limp. Both men were healed within an hour, but better friends because of it. The tension had been fought out of Tristan for the moment and Aaron got to see him as more of a human being, well, as human as a vampire could be.

That's how Mel found them twenty minutes later. Sitting at her little patio table near the pool, halfway to being drunk as skunks drinking her wine and singing at the top of their lungs. The song was about a Celtic battle and something to do with fair maidens, long boats, and dark nights. At least that's what she thought she'd heard.

"Well, where's your fair maiden, Tristan? I thought we were going to talk to her." She sat down and put her little basket of fruit on the table. Plucking out a pear, she began eating it, just as another pear appeared in its place in the basket.

"She flew away, she flew away. My fair maiden Bailey, she flew away." He was singing, he realized, and he wasn't even making sense to himself. He giggled again. Damn, what was in that wine?

"I think Tristan here is drunk. And he's floppy, err sloppy too. Hello, Mel, have you seen my mate? Tristan here smells like sex and I need to find Sara." He started to stand up, but sat back down.

Tristan looked to the sky again. He had screwed up again. Would he ever learn to not piss her off long enough to talk to her? "She's wounded again, Mel. She wouldn't let me see to them, just gave me a good fuck and fed me then left. She said that if I needed another one, I was to make arrangements with Griff." He turned to look at her. "I'm in love with her and she thinks all I want from her is sex and food."

"Yes, she does. And what are you going to do about that, Tristan?" Mel asked him softly.

He grinned then, not a pleasant grin, but one that looked full of malice and revenge. "Why, I'm going to kidnap her and tie her to the bed and have my wicked, wicked way with her. What do you think I'm going to do to her?"

~~~

Bailey went to their print shop with Griff the next morning. She had gone to Griff after leaving Tristan lying in the lawn in the magical realm. She had the ability to heal now that she had Tristan's blood in her, but it wasn't quick, nor was it without pain. Now her wounds took mere hours rather than days. The laceration on her leg was still seeping a small amount of blood, but it no longer pooled in her shoe. The burn was taking longer. It was still sore to the touch and movements of any kind made tears gather in her eyes. Griff had suggested that she take a few days off and get some rest. She agreed, and turned off her cell phone.

"They didn't take anything this time either, mistress. Just touched things and moved things about. The first one in the door will bear a mark that only you and I will be able to see. It will be a mark upon his forehead, a keyboard letter 't' for thief. I thought it would be appropriate. They will also have a marked need for the facilities. Their bowels will not hold anything for the next several days. I thought they should be easy enough to find that way. We shall just hide outside a restroom and wait."

She laughed, then thinking about her and Griff lurking around bathrooms waiting for them to come out again made her laugh harder.

Griff was a huge being. His head was an eagle, feathers of the darkest red and gold. His beak was long and sharp, pointing downward into a knifelike blade. His body was that of a very large, powerful wolf, the coat a hue so black it looked blue in the sunlight, and so soft, it felt like silk flowing through your fingers when you petted him. His tail was long, nearly the entire length of his body, and as strong as his legs and paws. There were wings along his back. Because of his weight, he was unable to use them to fly, but in a fight, they were deadly. Beautiful, as well, they were feathered in the same colors as his head, the colors blending into his furred coat to create the illusion that he wasn't winged, but coated in many colors and his fur rough. At the moment, he was wearing a headset, especially made to fit his small head.

"I think we'll wait a bit on the bathroom. I think it will be easier to track them if someone mentions a flu bug going around." She moved to the back room again and stopped.

Something was...well, not wrong, but off. She didn't spend a lot of time in this office to remember if things were missing or out of place, but in here, there was a difference. She moved out of the room physically, but mentally scanned it deeper. She was very patient and her skills honed to a perfect art. Moving along each inch of the room, she was able to find what she felt.

"Griff, there's a device in this room behind me. I don't know what it is, but it's in the upper left side of the ceiling. It's small, very, very small, so small I almost missed it. How do I get it without alerting them that we know about it?"

"There is the floor above us. We could go there. It may be where they inserted it from in the first place. I can feel it now. They did not enter that room when they were

here either time. Mistress, that is why I didn't find it. I'm truly sorry." He looked at her as if he were to blame for them entering at all. She loved this man very much.

"Don't be ridiculous, Griff, why would you search a room that hadn't been touched? I could just feel the hum of electricity, that's all. My senses are stronger than yours when it comes to that. I couldn't feel the magic hiding the magic. That's why we make a good team. Now, how do I get it out, or figure out how it got there?"

Griff could move through floors and walls and did so now, shifting himself to the room above them without being visible to anyone who may be there. He called for her to come up after about five minutes.

"They are not up there, but the rooms below are wired for this one. Whenever we enter the shop, there are cameras watching us. They are set up all along the floors into each of the rooms down here. All of them."

"The bathrooms too." It wasn't a question, and he didn't answer.

"Our computers seem to be wired to these, see this? As are all of our security cameras, which is another way they were able to get in and out." Griff nodded to the wall where a bank of computers were set up. On several were the views of the cameras at their doors and windows.

"I wonder how long, Griff. How long do you suppose they've been monitoring us and why?"

She looked at the expensive equipment and wondered who would have the monies it would require to set this up. She didn't think that this was their normal everyday criminal. She pulled out her cell phone and after turning it on, took several pictures of the set up. She immediately turned it off again before it rang.

"They know everything we do, mistress. Everything."

She moved about the room, slowly this time, and planned. Griff stood still; he knew not to disturb her. She sniffed and touched, then tasted at different points in the rooms, never saying anything.

"There's a wolf and vampire among the two humans. The humans haven't been here in a very long time, their scent old and faded. There have been as many as three male wolves, and only one vampire. Female. I've not scented them before, have you?" She turned to him now. The room was now cataloged as well as any librarian's books.

"No, none of the scents are familiar to me. The computers, they are expensive, as are the wires. I can see where they come from, but I don't see that as much help."

"I've got pictures and I think I might know someone who can help us to identify the way it's set up. I think that, like murders, hackers have their own set of ways of doing things. The building will need to be destroyed, any ideas?" She grinned at him, knowing that for as many ideas she could come up with to demolish the building, he had already discarded twice that many.

"Oh, I have a plan or two. When shall it happen?" He looked about the room again. "We will need to do it soon if we want to make sure that things are not found to be disturbed. I have all the necessary compounds to make it work."

"Tonight, if possible. Two days at the very latest. Do what you need to do to make sure no one is hurt, please."

They moved back to the room below and acted as though nothing had happened. A small glitch, a loss of power, would explain the few minutes that she had erased from their tapes.

CHAPTER THIRTEEN

The building blew the next afternoon. It was all over the news how a prominent printing firm had gone up in flames. Seven fire engines were called in to battle the blaze, yet it was considered a total loss. The new crew on site had been rerunning the same sound bite for over six hours.

A cleaning crew had come in to clean carpets on the second floor, readying it for new tenants, when the carpet cleaner had sparked and threw a flame up the curtain in one of the back rooms. The older building didn't stand a chance. Thankfully, everyone got out alive and no one was injured, thanks to the fast thinking of one of the cleaning crew women. The building, however, was a total loss. The owner of the building, out of the country at this time, couldn't be reached for comment.

Bailey was in Europe on a job. She had been hired by the alpha to take out six wolves that had killed two male American tourists. She was also supposed to help them find the missing two females that had been with them.

One of the women was a famous artisan, one who worked in clay and was quite wealthy.

She had stopped to make a purchase in a drug store when she heard a couple of Americans talking on their cell phone about the horrible fire and the explosion. She reached out to Griff immediately.

"Nice blaze, buddy. I like that you did it during the day. As one the owners of the building, could you see that the cleaning crew is not held accountable for the damages? And see that the woman is rewarded, please."

"It was my pleasure, I assure you." He laughed at her complement. *"I did find out about the rooms above us. The lease was in place when we purchased the building. I had forgotten that it was there. It was a ninety-nine year rent controlled, and it was held for another fifty-two years. The name on the lease is Charles Wolff, and was to be used as a storage area for files. The filing cabinets were moved out sometime ago and into a storage facility that was built on pack property."*

"I take it he hasn't been mentioned in any of the reports the news has been running. Where is our esteemed Charles Wolff now?"

Bailey had heard of Charlie, but had never had any direct contact with him. He was well respected and when he had stepped down several years ago, it was because he wanted to spend time with his mate, not because of any scandal. She had a feeling that he was not involved, but stranger things had happened.

"He is no longer on his vacation, but staying at the pack house proper. He and his mate have had a house built on the back of the compound and have lived there for

*two years. It is said that his grandson, Bradley Wolff has
lost his bitch and that the grandfather is there to keep him
company."*

*"I'll go and see what I can find out when I return in a
few days. In the meantime, we'll need another building.
Take out an ad in the paper and tell folks we are still open
for business. Make sure that it says that we aren't closed.
We can't afford to lose momentum now on what's going
on."*

Bailey wanted to ask if Tristan had contacted him, but
didn't want to be disappointed when he answered no. She
wanted Tristan in the worst kind of way, but a permanent
relationship wasn't something she could consider. She
decided that from now on, he would get only what he
needed, then maybe he'd get the hint and go to the queen
to have this taken care of.

After catching up on a few other matters, they closed
the connection. Bailey had to move on. Her targets were
on the go and she needed to keep up with them. One was
to lead her to another three on her list. Six targets at once
were getting to be the norm, and she wasn't all that happy
about it. It was difficult and stressful, not to mention
dangerous.

She was perched on a roof top watching the scene play
out below her when Tristan reached out to her.

"Bailey, I need you. Where can I meet you?" His
voice sounded hard and cold.

*"I'm going to be in Rome for a few more days, and
then I don't know where this one will lead me. If all you
need is one or the other, I can meet you in an alley
somewhere close. But both would take a little more time*

than I can spare while hunting." She knew it was cold and heartless, but she needed to move on with her life so that he could.

"I would like both, but a feeding will be fine. Are you free now?" Her heart hurt with his tone, and she didn't understand why. She knew that this was what she wanted.

"I have a target now, and it will be at least another hour before this is completed. I can meet you at the corner of Alley and James Streets at six-thirty Rome time. There's a dark alley there and no one will disturb you." She clamped her mind down and forgot about watching the street, but flew out over the city to get away from them all even for only a few minutes.

~~~

He was standing there waiting when she came around the corner. She was late, but only by three minutes. It might not have seemed so long had he not of been there since five-forty-five waiting for her, searching each face as it went by him.

"Tristan. There are two areas you can go, either is fine by me. I can pull shadows around us if you'd rather just eat here."

He noticed that she didn't look at him, but over his shoulder or the ground. How had they gotten to this point? It had been six days, and he was hungry, not just for her blood, though that was enough, but he wanted her body too.

"Bailey, please look at me."

When she didn't, he touched her chin and brought her face up to his. She had lost weight, he could see that immediately, and she had dark circles beneath her eyes.

He wondered if she was still injured and though he couldn't smell any blood on her, he just didn't know.

"Just get it over with, please. I have to be in France in an hour. And I still have things I need to get done before I leave."

She pulled away from his hand and leaned back against the building, exposing her neck to him. His hunger for her nearly overwhelmed him. He leaned into her quickly and licked the pulse beating there, her life blood tickling his tongue, her pulse beating hard against his mouth. Pulling them deep into the shadows so as no one would see them, he bit, deep and hard.

His first pull on her throat hardened his cock to the point of pain; the second swallow had him pressing her against the building, seeking relief that only she could give him. Tristan cupped her breast in one hand and cupping her ass in the other, pulled her tight against him. Still, he drank. He felt her graze her teeth across his neck, then lick the area with her hot, wet tongue. He was close, so close to stripping her down and taking her right there. If she bit him now, he knew that he would. But she didn't. She pulled her face away from his neck and let him drink his fill.

When he sealed the wounds and stepped back, he looked at her again. She had her face turned away from him again. He wanted to talk to her, to tell her how sorry he was, how much he needed her, but she stepped away from him in more ways than physically.

"Bailey, we can't go on like this. You have to realize that." He reached to touch her, to pull her into his arms. But she moved beyond him.

"I have to go to France. Please contact Griff when you need another meal." She shifted so suddenly that he was startled by the abrupt change. She was suddenly a large grey tabby running along the sidewalk close to the buildings.

CHAPTER FOURTEEN

She was looking at another building and was surprised when her phone rang. The only people who had this number were the queen and the one who served her. Neither Griff nor she used phones, and neither did Tristan.

"Hello?"

"I have a contract I'd like fulfilled immediately. I'm willing to pay a substantial bonus if it is done within the next seventy-two hours." She didn't recognize the voice. The voice modulator negated that anyway, but she did listen for clues that always gave the caller away.

"This is a printing shop; we don't do contracts. And we are temporarily out of business until we can set up another location. I'm sorry for your inconvenience, but I have the name of other..."

"Bullshit! I know what you are and what you do. Now you will do as I say. I will send you the things you need to kill this man. You also should understand that there are consequences if you don't. Understand me?"

Bailey understood just fine and disconnected the line. When it rang again, she let it go to voice mail.

When she picked up the message after she finished going through the building, it was to hear about a select few of the contracts she had fulfilled over the past six months. There was information on who, where, and how much she had been paid to do each hit. There were also references to her relationship with Tristan and to the Kiss of Aaron MacManus. She was given a phone number to call immediately or everything would go to the media, and then she could see how she handled that. She contacted Griff to trace the number and her phone, and then she dialed the number.

"This is the Printer, who is this?" She asked, knowing that whoever it was might not answer. But some people were incredibly stupid when asked a direct question and she was hoping for that.

"I'll do the talking, and you, you will do the listening. In less than one hour after we disconnect, you will get an email giving you all the information you need to do this hit. I expect it to be done without any problems, or you contacting anyone else except for your freak you have working for you. If I even hear of a whisper that you have, I will kill you."

"You think it will be that easy? Better yet, what makes you think I'll even care whether or not you kill me?" She didn't really, but lately, just lately, there seemed to be a little more to look forward to. She wasn't going to say it was Tristan, but she was beginning to look forward to him contacting her for his next meal.

"Then I will hit closer to your black heart. Tristan will die; I will take his head and make it look like you were the one to murder him. His family is royalty; do you think they'll be happy with just your death? Their money and connections alone will be able to hunt you for years. No, they will make you suffer in ways you cannot imagine. Do the hit, or else."

"Fuck off. I work for myself, and about Tristan? Are you fucking kidding me? I'm his food source, nothing more to him. He can barely stand to be in the same room as me." The scream that came through the line had her pulling the phone away. Bailey was surprised by that, and made a mental note to think about it later with the other information she was writing down about the call.

"Food source? You're his fucking mate, his mate for all time. He will die without you to feed him. I will not tolerate you belittling him again. If his death won't bother you then I will take out the precious mate of the master MacManus and his two brats. Let's see how long you live with their deaths hanging around your skinny little neck."

First she was willing to kill Tristan, now she didn't want her to belittle him. It was the children that got her, though. Children were innocents. Bailey had no doubt that this was a woman now. And she would be someone close to Tristan and the Kiss. Keeping her talking proved to be fairly easy as she was a gabby sort of thing.

"I'm no one's mate, not now, not ever. And if you think Tristan gives one shit about me then you're nuttier than a fruit cake. You send your contract, and if I decide to take it, I will. I don't care about the media, or anything else you think you might be able to blackmail me with. Bring it on, girl." She disconnected the line and snapped the phone in two, removing the battery as well. With a quick look around, she dropped it on the ground and sent a small bolt of energy to it, firing it on the spot. There was a slim possibility that she was as good as Bailey was, but she doubted that.

"Griff, we have a problem. Let me know if you receive anything via email about a rush job. I'm sure I just heard from one of the people who had us tracked. Did you get anything on the trace?" She was calm, but pissed.

"Yes, mistress. Right away. I couldn't trace the location, but the tracer picked it up as being local. It is a toss-away like the ones we generally use. As for the caller, did you get anything? Oh and the building you are in is ideal for what we need. There are already lines going in and the basement is finished. What would you like for me to do?"

"Buy it, but haggle. I can see that it needs some work, but very little. There aren't close enough neighbors to disturb us, but see what we can do about purchasing them as well. I don't want to take any more chances. And we are not going to honor anymore leases. Contact me as soon as you get the contract and it printed up. And other than a female who may or may not have connections to the Kiss that Aaron MacManus is currently master of, I got a few phrases that I might be able to track. Also, I caught some jealously for Tristan St. James. See if we can find a jilted lover or two for him as well." She wasn't going to think about how much it was hurting her to think he may have someone who wanted him back and would kill to have him.

The contract came in twenty minutes later; the money was not as much as she would normally get, but the bonus more than made up for the difference. It was the name on the contract that stunned her. She had just been hired to kill Bradley Wolff, alpha wolf.

Two hours later, Bailey was back in the realm hiding in the shadows waiting for the queen to make an appearance. She had been waiting for nearly an hour when Mel walked passed her. Reaching out, Bailey spoke to her.

"You need to leave this area and go to a secure location for me to speak to you. I have an issue that concerns you and yours, the children of Sara and Aaron MacManus for one. There are eight men currently residing in your infirmary that Griff and I sent there because of a breach in security on our end. They are connected. You have a breach in your security, your grace, and it may be the death of your family. Will you meet me?"

"Yes. There are beings here who can track you even now. Let me wait for my father. He can shield you and I won't need to use any traceable magic."

They waited in the hall, Mel looking at the floral arrangements with an assistant going over the colors and fussing with them. Bailey just waited, not giving a good fig if the white ones were too close to the yellow ones or not. And who even cared if the roses were better-looking next to the lavender.

She looked around the open field outside the doorway and noticed for the first time that there were fields and fields of wildflowers, all of them in neat patches according to color, type of flower, and height. She smiled and thought that Tristan would love this, all the neat little patches. It was like a big, organized blanket. Her smile didn't last long, though, thinking what a mess she was and how he was forever trying to neaten her up. Maybe the woman who was on the phone was just as organized as he was and they were a better match.

"Daddy, I was wondering if we could take a ride. It's such a beautiful day and I need a break." He had come when she had called for him, only knowing that she needed a shadow deeper than she could make without drawing attention.

They saddled up and rode out and away from the grounds twenty minutes later. Bailey hid in the mane of the larger horse as a barn mouse, hoping that no owl decided to make a snack out of her.

~~~

"I agree with Bailey on this, love. No one else should know. If too many people are aware, especially since she is sure that it is someone who knows the house, then the children are a risk as well. No, she's right."

Mel's dad had been brought in simply because he wasn't budging without knowing why he had been pulled from his computer. He was so intrigued by the Internet and all he could find.

"But there are already at least nine others involved, all against Bailey." Mel looked down at the little mouse on her horse. "No offense, but can you handle that many people at once?"

Mel just couldn't imagine why anyone would want Bradley dead. He was a good man and his family had been caring for the Brotherhood of Gray for several generations.

"If we play this right," Bailey said through their link. "Then we can catch all the players involved and the ring leader as well. If there is even a hint of what we are doing, the whole thing falls apart and Bradley ends up dead anyway."

"What of the ones we now have? What do I do with them knowing that they are in on this contract? I can't just let them go without punishment." Mel was worried about what would happen if they escaped to the human realm. "They have disobeyed direct orders of this kingdom concerning humans."

Bailey had told her how they had broken into the offices above her print shop, gathering information about her and the others she had worked for, and how she was now being blackmailed for the hit. She had also explained why she thought it was a woman calling the shots and not a man. Mel had the guard just outside the infirmary, but not with them yet, explaining that with that many people sick at once, she didn't want to run the chance of it being a plot against her.

"Nothing. If you do, then you will alert the leader or they will. You have to trust me on this, your grace, I know what I'm doing. Anything we do from this point on will be watched, and not only will it be watched, but someone may lose their life if we screw up."

Mel could hear Bailey's frustration. She knew the girl was right, but that didn't make it any easier to take. People were going to be killed; she had no doubt about that. It was the people who may be killed that had her terrified. And she couldn't do a damned thing about it. "So tell me the plan. I want to know every last detail."

Bailey groaned and James flopped back onto his back. This was going to be a long morning.

CHAPTER FIFTEEN

"I swear, where I'm taking him, no one will be able to feel his presence and no one can breach the area. He will be safe." Bailey had said this same thing a total of twenty-three times since sunrise. Her head hurt, she was tired, and she just wanted to be left alone to be able to do her job.

"I know you're frustrated. I can feel that, but do you realize what is going to happen once everyone thinks that he is dead? They are going to come for you, and when they do, I can't help you because you made me promise to stay out of it. Damn it, Bailey, what do I tell Tristan?"

Bailey looked up sharply and saw the look of *oh shit* on Mel's face. "What do you mean, what do you tell Tristan? Have you been talking with Tristan? About me?" Her heart rate picked up fast, and her mind was dizzy with the things she could be telling Tristan about her. "Your grace, what have you been telling Tristan?"

"He came to me through Sara. It was just after you told him what you were. He was upset and didn't know what to do about you. We wanted to help him." Mel shifted again.

"So you and Mrs. MacManus, what, gave him advice? Told him how to tame me? What?" Bailey was hurting. These women, they had helped Tristan, and he now had a woman willing to kill for him. Maybe she was going about this all wrong. Maybe the queen was part of the plot to get her killed.

"For the sake of all the Fates, you don't really believe that, do you? Why would I try and have you killed? You are a value to us. We need your skills."

If the queen thought she was helping, thought Bailey, she was so wrong. These people had been in her life since the beginning, she just realized. Tristan being able to contact her by her cell phone, him knowing where she was at all times. Things were beginning to fall into place and Bailey wasn't at all happy about it. She had a fleeting thought that maybe they had arranged her to meet him but dismissed that immediately. No, the Fates had done that; otherwise Bailey wouldn't have this strange connection with him. But it still smacked of interference from this woman.

"When this is over, and if I live, I will never do another contract for you again. Never. You should have kept your mouth shut and out of my business." Bailey gathered her things from the room and left the castle. Mel's pleading followed her all the way out into the human world.

~~~

"Fine Printing, may I help you?"

"Griff?" Tristan had been trying to contact Bailey for several hours. He wasn't worried, not yet at any rate. She could block him when she was working. He didn't like it, but he was trying hard to understand. But now, he needed her.

"This is Fine Printing, may I help you?" Tristan noticed that the voice had gotten harder.

"It's Tristan St. James, Bailey's mate. I'm trying…she told me to contact you if…I was trying to find her. Do you, can you tell me where she is?" It was like Oliver Twist begging for more, please, he thought. Damn it, what the hell had gone wrong?

"My lord. Yes, my mistress is here. We are setting up the new offices. The equipment arrived a few hours ago and the men have gone now."

"I couldn't reach her. She's blocked…I mean, can she come to the phone?" Tristan was hungry. He'd waited nearly two weeks this time. It was childish on his part, he knew, but he also knew that if he saw her, they'd argue and he didn't want that either.

"That is my fault, my lord. I've taken the liberty of warding the building so that no one will know when we are in residence. It seemed much safer after the last time. She is here, but I am loath to wake her. She has not been sleeping well." Tristan could hear the tone in his voice, and felt that he had deserved it.

"I need to see her, Griff. Do you know when she might be rising? I could come to her if that would help. I don't want to take her from her work."

That wasn't true. He wanted to take her from everything. He wanted to hide her away and have his way with her until she was too sated to work. Then when he was rested, start all over again.

151

"She has been sleeping soundly for about twenty hours now, sire. As I said, she has not been sleeping well and what little sleep she gets seems to be fitful and not restful. Also, I believe she needs to feed as well. She has been a little slower of late."

Tristan's whole body froze. Bailey needed to feed? No, he couldn't have heard him correctly. He leaned his head against the wall were he stood. He calmed his voice as he asked again. "Did you say she needs to feed? Griff, does Bailey need to feed like I do?" Chanting in his head was, *no, no, no.*

"Yes, my lord. Not as often, I believe, as you do, but she needs to feed at least once a week. More if she is hurt or weak. It is my understanding that she can no longer feed from anyone but you, am I correct?"

Tristan heard the panic in Griff's voice and would have calmed him, but his own was rising. She was asleep and had been for nearly twenty-four hours. She was shutting down and he knew it. If she didn't get some blood soon then—

"Griff, I need you to go and see if you can wake her. Give me the address and I will be there in seconds, but try and wake her." Tristan was terrified. "Griff? Please keep her safe until I can get there. Please?"

"Yes, my lord. I shall. I am sorry. I did not think...I had assumed she was getting her nourishment from you."

"I'm coming. I'll be there very soon." Tristan closed his eyes and willed himself there. He was outside the building within moments. He had to pound on the door for several more because he couldn't come in without an invite, both the wards and being a vampire preventing him from entering.

Griff granted him access and he went to her. She was weak and her body had started conserving, shutting itself down when food wasn't replacing what she used. The deep sleep had been necessary and had replenished her somewhat.

"You fool!" he screamed at her when she opened her eyes. "You nearly scared ten years off my life!" Tristan was mad, no longer as scared as he had been now that he could see that she was alive. He shook her hard, and he could swear he heard her teeth rattle together. She smacked his hands away weakly.

"Stop that, I'm fine." She pulled away from him, only to stagger slightly. "So what. I forget to stop at Mickey D's, so sue me. It's not like I haven't been a tad busy the past few days."

"You haven't fed. You haven't fed in nearly three weeks, and I know as well as you do that whatever the fuck Mickey D's is isn't going to cut it. You should have fed from me. Me, damn it." He found himself pacing. He never paced, and made himself sit down.

"Oh, and who the fuck have you been feeding from? Huh? Got yourself a little snack and fuck somewhere else? I've been busy!" He was stunned to see her fangs. Her eyes had turned as well. Need, incredible need, slammed into him, making the beast in him surface and snarl for release.

He leapt from the chair and had her pinned against the wall in seconds. They were both breathing hard, their hearts pounding. He could feel it now, her hunger. His need jumped to a new level.

Tristan put his hands to her throat and his fingers against her pulse. Slowly, he ran his fingers down the long column of her neck and touched the collar of her t-shirt as it rested on both of her shoulders. His eyes were blazing when he met hers.

"Bailey, I want you. I want to make love to you, in a bed. I want to feel your body surrounding mine while I'm deep inside of you, your heat wrapped around me. I want to bury my cock into your pussy while you ride me and come on me, with me. Then I want to feed from you. I want to have you sink your teeth into my flesh and drink and long from me."

He pulled the shirt apart, ripping it from the collar to the hem. He looked down at her breasts, heaving now, cupped in a bright orange bra that barely contained their bounty. He hooked his finger in the front of it, extended a single claw, and sliced it open. Tenderly, he pulled the opening apart and she spilled from the confining material.

Her breasts tightened and her nipples hardened as he gazed at them. His mouth watered and his fangs elongated, his need to taste, to bite, strong; his need to worship stronger.

"Touch...I want you to touch them." He watched as her hands moved up her ribs slowly to just under the weight of her. Cupping her hands, she lifted them up and brushed her thumbs across the tight nubs of her nipples. Her moan shot through him, shot need straight to his cock.

"Tristan, I...what do you want me to do? I've never...I want to...it feels good." She pushed them together and using her thumb and finger, gently pinched her left nipple and then rolled it between her fingers.

He bent his head and captured the right nipple with his lips, nibbling hard, biting but not breaking skin yet. When she arched her back and bowed toward him, he pulled back and stepped away. "No, not this time. I'm not taking you against the wall like an animal again. I want you beneath me, not writhing against the wall." And he took another step back.

Tristan picked her up in his arms and when her bare breasts rubbed against his shirt, he felt the heat as though she were touching his bare skin.

"Where is your bed, Bailey? I don't care if it's halfway around the world, we are going to make love in a proper bed." After three tries of her voice not working, she gave him her address. They were there in seconds.

He sat her down on her feet next to the big bed. Of course it wasn't made, but right now he didn't care. All he could think about was her, her body, and them.

"Help me undress. But we're going to go slowly. We have all night. And I plan to spend it inside of you."

He watched as she brought her shaking hands up to his tie and worked at the knot. When she was shaking so badly she couldn't undo the buttons, he wrapped his hands over hers just to calm her. When he felt them work easily again, he slid his hands down her arms and encircled her tiny waist.

"I want to...can I taste your skin, Tristan? I want to lick your skin and taste you." Her fingers running through the hair on his chest were hot and making him hotter with her tentative touches and caresses. "Your blood is so hot to me, and when I taste your skin on my tongue, it's everything I can do not to take a bite of you."

"I want you to do what you need, what you feel. I'm as much yours as you are mine. Touch me, Bailey, taste me. I'm certainly going to do the same to you."

Her fingers toyed with his nipple until he thought he'd scream, and then she ran her tongue around the dark areola before taking it into her mouth and sucking. When he hissed his approval, she pulled away. Cupping her head, he pulled her back. A frown furrowed her brow.

"Christ, don't stop. Please, don't stop. I love your mouth on me. The way your tongue heats my flesh everywhere it touches me. I want you to bite me, Bailey, bite me hard."

He felt her teeth scrape against his swollen peak, then her tongue rasped wetly over it before she sank her fangs deep into him. His growl was deep, rumbling through his chest and out his mouth. He let her drink from him there, let her taste her first of many bites he hoped they'd share tonight.

He pulled her to his body and crushed her breasts to him. Cupping her ass, he pulled her tighter against his cock and rode her up and down him while she continued to caress his body. When she wrapped her legs around him, he lowered them to the bed, him nestled between her thighs.

"Please, our pants, we need...oh, Tristan I want you inside of me." She wrapped her armed tighter around his neck as she moved harder into his groin.

"I want this to last. If I get you naked now, I won't be able to stop from entering you." He moved against her again, pushing into her and pressing her into the bed.

"Next time, you can make it last next time. Inside of me, please, Tristan. I really need to feel you inside of me. I want to feel your thick cock stretching me, filling me. I want to feel you touch me deep inside, then your cum, I want to feel your hot cum shooting inside of me, filling me. Please?"

He rolled to his back, stripped the belt from its loops, and had his pants down and off in nanoseconds. He was pulling hers down her legs and standing before her naked body mere seconds later. His cock was straining straight out from his body, hard, thick and hot. She licked her lips as she stared at him.

"Roll over." When she didn't move, but continued to stare at his now weeping cock, he picked her up and sat down with her across his lap. "You are going to pay for that, my dear. My control is nearly gone. Your disobedience must stop or you will face the consequences."

He was going to spank her. Actually spank her! She struggled to sit up, to get off his lap but he held her down and smacked his hand hard against her bare ass cheek. She stopped moving. He slapped again, harder this time.

"When I give you an order, I expect it to be obeyed without question, understand?" He rubbed the area he had hit as he spoke to her.

"Fuck you, you miserable prick"

He brought his hand down again, watching as his handprint reddened her pale skin. "Bailey, I mean it. I will spank you until you tell me you will obey me." He could feel her juices gathering on his thigh, and he slid his fingers beneath her. Gathering some on his fingers, he rubbed it into her reddened ass, smoothing and soothing as he went. He pulled his hand back and spanked again, harder this time.

She wasn't trying to get away now; she was rising up to meet his strikes. He could smell her arousal, heavy and thick around them. He moved in, gathered more of her cream, and moved it along the slit, opening it for his fingers.

Using his other hand to open her ass wider, he worked her hot juices into her anus, massaging and teasing it.

"Relax, Bailey, let me in, baby. I want to fuck you with my finger." He slowly inserted his long finger to the first joint, moving in and out, back and forth, then deeper and faster.

"Tristan, please, I need to come, please."

He didn't want to stop what he was doing, but if she came like this, he would as well. Pulling out of her tight hole, he moved her to his lap, her thighs spread over his.

"Bailey, I want you. I need you."

"Yes, I know." She pressed against him and he lifted her up and slowly slid her onto him. He lay back on the bed and with his hands on her hips, showed her how to ride him, slow and long movements.

"Tristan, I'm sorry, I'm hungry. Please, I need to…bite me, please. Let me feed from you." He sat up and moving her hair, and licked her throat. When she nuzzled deep into his shoulder, he bit hard and drank.

He flipped her over onto her back and she hooked her ankles around his hips. Riding her hard and fast, he tilted his head back, further exposing his jugular for her, and she bit him. His climax slammed into him, pushing him beyond all reason. He tore his mouth from her neck and let her drink her fill while he pistoned into her, her own climax triggering another from him.

CHAPTER SIXTEEN

He started filling her tub while she slept. He had been rough with her and wanted to soothe her in a warm bath. When the water was high enough where he thought they could both get in without flooding the downstairs bath, he went to get her.

"Bailey, honey, I ran us a bath. Come on, it'll make you feel better." He started to pick her up and she smacked him in the chest.

"Go away. I feel just fine right now." She rolled over onto her back and snuggled deeper into the blanket.

"Bailey, I'm going to pick you up." He put action to words, ripped the blanket off of her, and scooped her into his arms before she could get away. He was stepping into the tub when she finally squirmed around enough to have her chest pressed to his. Sinking down in the tub, she wrapped herself around him and sighed.

"Okay, you were right, this does feel better." She scooted around so that she lay against the other end of the tub across from him. He looked at her for long moments before he spoke.

"I didn't know you fed. Why didn't you say anything to me?" That had bothered him the most, that she had gone hungry rather than seek him out for food.

"I usually just feed from the targets if I'm hungry. I seldom get that way and when I do, I just feed. It's no big deal. But lately, I don't know, I haven't had the urge."

She began soaping up the large sea sponge with some scented liquid soap that was sitting on the edge. When she lifted her leg out of the water to wash it, he watched, mesmerized by something so mundane as washing.

"Has no one ever fed from you before?" The other leg came out of the water and the sponge moved down along the flesh. He reached out, took it from her, and began washing her foot.

"No, it was forbidden at the lab, not that anyone wanted to get that close to us. They told us what would happen if we did, so neither Tyler nor I ever did. At least I don't think he did. He may have with a lover or two. I never asked him." He pulled her toward him and turned her around to wash her back. He looked at the scars. She had there and he touched the larger one.

"What did this?" It was long, about five inches, and about an inch wide. There were stitch marks, little holes on either side of the wound. The stitches didn't look even, as though someone without any skill had put them there.

"Hummm, oh I think that one was from when Tyler and I were training. I think I was about four or five. I couldn't hold the blade very well and he got the jump on me. I hit the wall where the other weapons were stored and one of the pikes fell off its hanger and gouged me."

He kissed the scar, and then licked along it; he felt the shudder run along her skin.

"Who...who stitched it up?" He pulled her closer to his chest and poured more of the creamy soap on the sponge. After he lathered it up again, he began washing her arm, first the right, then the left. He washed her hands, each finger, then her wrists.

"Stitched? I don't...the scar. Tyler did. It was his punishment because he didn't kill me when he had the opportunity. He hated the sight of blood, and an open wound would make him puke. What are you doing?" Her breasts tightened under his ministrations. He could see how responsive they were from the sponge rubbing across them.

"Bathing you. Don't you like it? I like the smell of this. I bet this is why your skin is so soft." He moved it down beneath the water and ran it back and forth across her hips, slowly and gently.

"I don't wear scents often, I need to be hidden and a smell can...please stop. You're making me crazy." She took the sponge from him and turned around to face him. "I have to talk to you. You're not going to like it, but I don't have a choice."

"All right. Do we stay here, or would you like to tell me while we're dressed?" He wanted to talk to her too, and he also knew she wasn't going to be happy with him either.

"Dressed. That way, if you want to leave, which you will, there will be no awkward moments while you dress." She stood up, reached for one of the towels folded on the side of the tub, and handed it to him. She pulled the other to her, flipped it open, and wrapped it around her body. Stepping from the tub, she moved on into the bedroom beyond. By the time he was dried and his own towel was around him, she was gone.

One of his powers was to manifest clothes he or someone he was touching might need. He was also able to remove them with just as much efficiency. He hadn't removed their clothes even when they were nearly tearing at each other because he found that exciting. He should try that on her one of these days and see how she liked that. He was still grinning when he entered the kitchen, where she was just closing her cell phone.

"I've ordered me a pizza; I assume you won't want any of it." She had her head in the refrigerator and wasn't looking at him.

"You would assume correctly. You should be eating more meat and drinking more fruit juices."

"And you should stop acting like a father. Nice duds." They were, too—navy blue silk shirt with a darker tie. The dress pants were a lighter blue and hung across his slim hips in a loving caress. "Do you ever wear anything but dressy clothes, not even jeans and a sweatshirt?"

"Bailey?"

"Okay. I have an assignment tomorrow. And in all likelihood, I'll be killed. I just thought you should know."

She didn't look at him. Not right away at least. He was pissed, shocked and pissed, but she wanted him to know. No, that wasn't it either. She needed him to know. And she hoped, stupidly, that he would listen to her as she explained.

"Well, isn't that just great of you," he snarled at her. "Thank you so much for the heads up."

She was trying to be truthful and he was actually snarling at her. Bailey took several deep breaths to calm herself. She wished that she could give him details, but he, out of all the people that would be affected by this, needed him to be the one that would be unharmed.

"It's…I want you to go to Griff if you need anything. He knows your scent now and he'll let you in any of the buildings we own jointly. He can't go into public for reasons I'm sure you can guess, so someone will need to make sure things are taken care of for him."

"So, what, Bailey, that's it? I'm going to be killed and, oh, by the way, take care of my friend once I'm dead? What am I supposed to do? Any last words of advice for me? What the hell is going on?"

She turned away from him and looked at the mess in the living room. She didn't want to answer him, but knew that she had no choice. "I…this assignment, this target…I probably won't be coming back. No, that's not true either. I won't be coming back. The danger is…in all likelihood, I'll be dead. I'll be killed by either hi…the target or those who wish to avenge his death." It didn't sound any better saying it out loud than it did in her head, she thought.

"Are you saying you *plan* on getting yourself killed?" His voice cut through her and straight to her heart. He couldn't possibly believe that, she hoped.

"I'm not planning it, no, but it's a good probability that I will. I mean, I've been in dangerous situations before, but this one is different. The players are different.

The demands are...Tristan, this isn't what I want, but I have no choice."

"Yes you do, Bailey. Everyone has a choice. Just say no; don't do it. In fact, if it helps, tell them I said no."

He stood there glaring at her with his arms crossed over his chest. It that very moment, she realized that she was in love with him. Her heart shattered in her chest. She'd found love only to have to toss it back because of circumstances. Well fuck a duck.

"It doesn't work that way and you know it. I have to do this. If I don't, someone else will and it won't be all right...I mean, things could go wrong and he could...I take my job very seriously."

She turned from him to get her cash from the kitchen drawer. She could smell the food coming up the stairs to her floor and she wanted to hustle the kid out fast. Bailey was walking toward the door when the bell rang.

"Hi Bail, didn't think you was gonna call this week. Bugs said you had a hot date and hot dates didn't need...oh, hi." Bailey turned around and saw Tristan leaning against the jamb of living room, glaring at Sammy the pizza boy.

"How much this time, Sammy?" She ignored Tristan and focused all her attention on what she was doing with her food. She didn't know why she asked the price. It was always the same. Apparently, Sammy was confused too because he was looking at her like she had asked him the formula for some chemical compound.

"Huh? Oh nineteen ten. Didn't know you had company. You shoulda told Bugs. He'd of added you another pie or something." Sammy kept looking over at Tristan, but Bailey refused to acknowledge him.

"Here you go, buddy. Keep the change. I'll see you around. Tell your mother I said hello." She practically slammed the door in his face, flipped the locks, and turned to go back into the kitchen.

"You do know you gave him a twenty dollar tip, don't you?" He followed her in and sat across from her when she opened the box and bit into the first slice. He got up and looked for a plate and finding no napkins, gave her several paper towels. She ignored the plate and used the box instead.

"You should try a slice. You might be surprised that you can eat again." She had polished off three slices in less than five minutes. The concoction smelled great and looked even better; it was covered in what could only be considered double the meat, cheese, and sauce.

He reached over, took the plate she had pushed aside, and slid a hot slice onto it. He got up and retrieved a fork and knife and more paper towels. After folding the towel in half, he laid it on his lap and picked up the utensils to eat. His glance at her had him stop in mid cut.

"What?" He looked completely out of his element. She didn't answer him, but shook her head and bit into her fifth piece.

They both finished off the pizza. Tristan ate eight slices to her six, then surprise, surprise, he cleaned up the kitchen, washing the few things they had used and putting them away again. They were in the living room sitting on opposite ends of the couch when he picked up the conversation right where they left off.

"So, who do you have to call to get out of this?" She looked at him and was amazed again at her feelings for him. Love was very strange.

"Get out of what?" She ran her foot up his leg, over his knee, and back down again. The second time she went to his thigh, he opened his legs wider and scooted down more.

"The contract. Who do you have to call to…Bailey, stop it; I'm not in the mood right now." Which was a lie, she thought. She could see his cock lengthening, hardening through his pants.

"I'm not calling anyone. There isn't anyone to call." This time, she rubbed her foot across his balls, then up over his cock before moving back down his thigh and up again. He hissed at her and she pressed harder on him, curving her toes around his hardness.

"There has to be…don't do that. Bailey, I'm not kidding." He captured her foot this time and used it to rub hard against him, up and down.

"Take out your cock, Tristan. Let me see it." This was their last night, she thought. She wanted him to remember her.

~~~

Tristan set her foot on his thigh and opened his belt, then his button. He slowly pulled down the zipper and watched her stare at him as he worked the placket open. His cock sprang free of the opening as soon as he pulled his pants down passed his hips. He fisted his cock, up and down, and watched the change in her. Her need pooled in her eyes.

"You keep looking at me like that and I'm going to come just like this." His hand slowed and he loosened the tight hold he had on himself. He wanted this to last.

"I'd like that, to see you come. To see your hot cum shoot out of you. I'd like that very much." She had moved her hand down and was playing with her belly button with one finger while the others were skimming along the top of her pants.

"Take off your clothes, Bailey. I want to see you touch yourself again. That was perhaps the most erotic thing I've ever seen anyone do."

She stood up and pulled the t-shirt up and over her head, baring her breast with a small bounce for him. She turned back to him and with her thumbs hooked into her pants, turned her back to him and pushed them down to her knees, and then bent at the waist to take them off over her feet. Her ass was positioned in front of him, right in front of his face.

His heart rate doubled when she reached behind her and opened her ass cheeks for him, exposing the tiny rosebud to him while she was still bent over. Bringing one hand to the front of her, she spread her legs wider and inserted a finger into her dripping wet pussy. His eyes crossed when she brought her finger to her mouth, suckled it, and moaned.

"Turn around, turn around and lean over the couch." She walked around to the back of the couch and placed her hands on the back. She leaned down into it and spread her legs wide. He got up and moved up behind her, rubbing his cock in the juices that dribbled down her thighs.

"If you think this is going to make me forget what we were talking about, you're wrong. I'm going to make you pay for teasing me like this." He smacked her ass hard, bringing a small cry from her. He smacked her twice more, her ass bright red and he was sure burning.

He touched her pussy, gathered her cream onto his fingers, and opening her ass, began rubbing it into her bud. He didn't ease his finger in this time, but rammed it into her, deep and fast. He added a second finger too soon and nearly came when she moved back against his invasion after the initial assault. He kept his fingers working her, grabbed his cock with his other hand, and began working her cream from her pussy over the head.

"Bailey, I'm going to fuck this tight ass and it's going to hurt." He removed his fingers and moved his now drenched cock head to her entrance. Moving slowly against and away, he waited for her to answer him, all the while stretching her wide, opening her for him.

"Please, Tristan, please, fuck me."

He pushed the engorged head into her. She cried out but didn't pull away. He moved another few inches in and pulled back, then into her more. He did this slowly over and over until he was buried to the hilt. Sweat was pouring off him. He'd never worked so hard for something in his life, and it was worth every bit of it.

He stopped moving. As much as he wanted to fuck her now that he was inside of her, he didn't want to hurt her any more. Leaning into her, he reached around to her pussy and found her clit. She was swollen and the little nub was no longer covered by her nether lips but peeking out for his touch. He teased it with his fingers, and when she started to ride against him, he began to move inside of her again. The grip she had on his cock was tight to the point of near pain but he couldn't stop.

He was close, the heat and the tightness making it impossible for him not to shoot his load into her sooner than he wanted. Pinching her clit, he felt her contract tighter around him as she came, crying out his name over and over. He roared, his own climax seizing him quicker than it ever had as he rammed deep and emptied himself into her.

He couldn't move. He knew that his weight leaning onto her had to be too much, but he simply couldn't make his legs move to stand up, much less hold his own weight. He kissed her shoulder, tasting the salty sweat. Bath, they needed another bath. He wished he was home in his lair. The underground pool that he'd had the room built around would have been wonderful right now. But he didn't have the energy it would require to transport them both there. She had drained him. He chuckled out loud at that thought.

"If you can laugh, you can move." She started to move, to stand, but he wasn't ready to leave her body just yet. Pulling her hips back against him again, she moaned before she leaned back against his chest. "I don't think…I can't again, Tristan. I'm…I…"

"I know, love. I just wanted to hold you. I hurt you, I'm sorry. Next time it won't be so bad." She turned to him and brought her mouth to his for a gentle kiss, her back still pressed to him, his semi-hard cock still deep inside of her.

Pulling away and out of her, but not breaking the kiss, he bent over, picked her up in his arms, and carried her back in the bathroom. The water was still running, but he stepped into it and sat in the warm water. He held her tight against him and after a few minutes, he sat her up and began cupping water over her hair. When it was wet, he poured a good amount of shampoo into his hand and started working into her hair. Rinsing it proved a little tricky, but she gave him a plastic glass she had hidden among the plants around the tub. When he had finished washing her body, using more of her scented soap than necessary, he stood her up, set her outside the tub, and dried her off, moving the fluffy, thick towel over every inch of her body. Sitting down on the toilet, he sat her on his lap and began running his fingers through the tangles in her hair. When he had removed as many as he could, he picked up her comb and ran it through the long mass.

"No one's ever bathed me before. It's very decadent, isn't it?" They were in bed now, her in yet another pair of lounge pants and sleeveless tee. The pants were a strange-looking sponge in a pair of shorts and a sailor hat. The shirt was a picture of the same character, but he was swollen up with water while sitting in a tub.

"It can be if it's done correctly." He pulled her close to him and held her tight. He realized after a few minutes that she was asleep, her soft snores puffing against his bare chest. He yawned himself and pulled the blankets up and over them both. He inhaled her scent deep into his lungs, thinking that he would need to buy the company that made that particular soap; it would be so worth every penny of whatever they wanted. He fell asleep with a smile on his face and one in his heart.

CHAPTER SEVENTEEN

It was late afternoon when he woke up. He knew right away that she was gone, knew that she had gone on her assignment. He went into the bathroom and found her note to him.

"Thanks for making the bed," it started. He looked back into the bedroom and noticed that he had indeed made the bed, the linens in a pile at the foot and the fresh ones he'd found in her closet now on it. He started reading again.

"Thanks for making the bed. I knew you wouldn't be able to help yourself.

I've gone to take care of the target. I'm sorry you'll feel that I've disobeyed you, but I have no choice in this matter.

Griff has some things for you to sign and a few things I'd like for you to have. I don't have a lot, but it's all yours.

175

There will be some things said, most of it will be true, but I wanted you to know that I love you. I don't know how long I've known, it seems like all my life, but I love you.

When this is all over, please go to see the queen. She has something for you as well. Goodbye, my love.

Bailey St. James. "

~~~

"Where is she? I know you know, so tell me who the target is and where she is." He had stormed into the castle as soon as he left her apartment.

"I can't tell you and you damn good and well know that I can't. I also don't appreciate you slamming doors and acting like you own the fucking place. She said to come here when it's over. I don't have the energy to deal with you today. Go home." When she turned her back on him, he lost control. He leapt across the room and had her throat in his hands before her guard could react.

"They move and I will take this pretty head of yours off at the shoulders. The woman I love is out there somewhere and I want you to tell me where." She wasn't struggling against him, which should have been his first clue; his second should have been the buildup of power surrounding her. He was across the room and against the wall before he drew his next breath.

"The two of you need to learn protocol when it comes to touching me. I can't tell you where she is, Tristan. I can't break a promise. I would like to, but it's in my blood. Once I make a promise, I cannot break it." She had walked over to where he sat on the floor.

"She's out there, she's in trouble, and I can't help her. I need her, Mel. I need her more than I've ever needed

176

anything in my life. Not just for blood, but her. I love her." He hadn't even bothered getting up, but sat slumped on the floor in a pile of wood that had once been a Louie the Fourteenth chair.

"I wish that I could help you, I truly do. She needs to finish this, Tristan. There isn't any way for her not to. Others will die if she doesn't." Mel took his hand in hers. "Like me, once a promise is given, she cannot break it. She left you something, your freedom. She bargained for your life before she left. When she dies, you will be free of the bond you have with her. You will no longer be her lifemate. She wanted you to be able to live on without her."

"She thinks that's all it takes? Just a little magic and I won't need her anymore?" He wouldn't believe she thought so little of him, so little of his feelings for her. "I love her, don't you get it? I fucking love her. I don't think I've loved anything as much...she's my life, all of it. Without her, my life isn't just meaningless, it's not worth living. I would rather meet the sun than to go a day without her."

"Tristan, did you tell her that you loved her? Does she know what you just told me, that you love her with all your heart? That you've loved her for a very long time?"

He hadn't, he realized. He'd never once told her that he loved her. He had called her his love plenty, but never once had he said the words, those three little words.

"I see that you haven't. Then why should she think any differently than she does? Your freedom is granted. The moment she dies, you will be free of your bond with her and able to feed as you had before meeting her. And don't even think about meeting the sun, bucko. You already fixed that little out. You can walk in the daylight, eat food, and everything else she can do. Once her blood mingled with yours, your fate was sealed." She sat down on the sofa and stared at him. "And just so you know, I love the twit as well. Damn her for putting me in this position."

"I need to find her. Please, tell me how I'm going to find her." Before he could plead with her any more, Sara stormed into the room in much the same way he had only moments before.

"You are not going to believe what's just happened!! The Printer, Bailey, has killed Bradley Wolff, killed him right in front of half a dozen people."

CHAPTER EIGHTEEN

Bradley woke and knew immediately he was in wolf form. He also knew that he was deep within the earth, the smell of soil teasing his senses. Raising his muzzle, he sniffed the air, blood and lots of it. Some of it was his, he realized, but not all.

"You can shift at anytime. She had to pull your wolf to expedite your healing process." The voice was deep and accented, Celtic, he thought, somewhat like his friend Colin's.

"I should like to meet him one day," the voice beyond the darkness said. "If that is possible after this is over. It is always nice to meet one's clansman. Yes, I can read your mind. It is the only way I have been able to survive this many years. Shift, please. I have human food for you and when you are ready. I will light the room."

Bradley shifted and had to sit down. He was weak and sore. His body felt abused and he was sure that if he could see it, it would be bruised. He hurt in more places than he thought he had parts for.

"Where..." His throat was sore and tight. "Where am I?"

"You are in the belly of a cave, deep within the mountains of the Netherlands. A friend of my mistress has given you shelter for now. Your throat, its soreness will dissipate soon. Are you ready to remember what transpired?"

Bradley wasn't sure, but he didn't like the fog that he felt either. He was almost afraid to ask what he didn't remember, and then chuckled. He supposed that was the point, wasn't it? He nodded to the voice across the room.

And just like that, he suddenly remembered what had happened. It came crashing into him like a rolling boulder down a hill, picking up more and more as it went, speeding its way to the bottom. He had to put his head between his legs when the realization hit him about why he was here.

"She...that girl, she tried to kill me." He moved then, and tried to sit up. He felt clothes hit his chest and the scent of blood increase. Someone else, a female, had entered the room. And she was injured.

"I did kill you, as a matter of fact. Griff saved you." She sat down hard on something. Her body sliding down the wall made him look to where she was. "Hello, Bradley, I'm the Printer, Bailey Morrison. This is my friend Griff. Please don't be alarmed by him. He won't hurt you. Griff, lights, if you please." The room lit with hundreds of candles at different places around the cave.

He noticed the creature first. He was huge and wide. A Cynogriffon, if memory served him. Then he saw the woman, a girl really. She was sitting on the floor, huddled in the corner near a pool of water. And she was bleeding very badly. Bradley, not shy about his nudity, stood up slowly and began to dress.

"Why?" His throat hurt, and talking strained it, so he used as little of it as he could.

"I guess you deserve to know. You should also know that it's not over yet. I'm sorry, but you'll need to remain here for a few more days. I should…Griff will take you home as soon as it's safe." She nodded toward the creature and he left them alone. "Several days ago, a female vamp called in a hit. At first I refused it, not even knowing who the target was. But she had information, and details that she could only have gotten from compromising my offices and computers. A lot of information."

"So you took the hit to save your own ass? How very noble of you." Bradley sat down and pulled the tray of covered food toward him, hunger making his belly growl. "So this was all a ploy to get money. You are a piece of work, aren't you?"

"You're still alive, pup, and you'd do well to keep a civil tone in your head when talking to my mistress." Griff had pounced when he had returned and now stood over Bradley, his massive paw pressing hard into his chest. "I have not decided you are worthy of her death yet."

"Griff, it's okay" Bailey said. "He has every right to be pissed. But I would prefer, alpha, if you would keep a civil tone. Griff and I aren't the only ones that are in this mountain. No, I didn't do it to save my ass, but others, the master of his realm and his family being just a few. The information wasn't about me, but about the people I've worked for. The queen is…was one of my employers, as were many other beings. Over the years, I've completed many hits for her, both magical and human. Your father was another person I worked for."

"You lie! My father was a good man, and has been dead for nearly ten years. He would never stoop so low as to hire someone like you to kill another person for him." He struggled to stand, but Griff simply growled a warning.

"Does the name August Sheppard ring a bell? I was hired to just target him, to gather information on him and bring it back to your father. Bradley Senior thought Sheppard was into drugs, selling to the younger pack members and making a profit. It wasn't until I was on his tail for several days that I found it went much deeper than that." Bailey shifted on the rock and continued her tale. "He was also selling the younger females, some wolf and some human, to another country to be used as prostitutes. I couldn't come back and let your father know about the crime without leaving the others still at his mercy. The young girls with him were dying. So I killed him. Cut his throat and freed the women. Several days later, before I could let Bradley Senior know what had happened, he was killed in that car accident with your mother."

Bradley did remember something about the man and his father's involvement. He had been killed not long after the grisly discovery was made. There had been ten young women dead in an abandoned building on the estate, and twenty more starved and ill. It had taken weeks to get them home again, some of the deceased never claimed.

He looked at the woman before him. That had been over ten years ago. She didn't look any older than some of the pups in his pack. She could have only been in her mid to late teens when she had done this for his father. Then something occurred to him.

"Were my parents' deaths in any way connected to this Sheppard?" He had never thought of the two being connected before, but now that he did, he was terrified of her answer.

"No," she told him, sorrow evident in her voice. "Your parents' deaths were just as it was thought, an accident. I looked into it personally just be sure." He heard her moan deep and then Griff move to her side.

"You're bleeding. What's happened?" He stood now, but Griff blocked him from getting close to her.

"Your brother is a good shot. I...he was armed and I didn't see it until too late. He couldn't harm Griff or you wouldn't have survived." She moaned again, and the smell of fresh blood permeated the air.

"How bad is it?" Bradley knew it was bad. He could hear her heartbeat and it wasn't strong. If she didn't get medical treatment soon, she'd die. He realized that they both knew this as well. He looked at Griff and the other man shook his head sadly.

"Sit down, alpha. I don't have a lot of...I need to explain to you why you were targeted. You have to tell...The contract was to take you out, kill you within seventy-two hours or she would kill Tristan. But I didn't bite at that. Something in her voice told me that she wouldn't hurt him. But then she targeted the MacManus children and the adults. While I don't know them, contrary to popular belief, I'm not so cold hearted as to have children die, even by my hand indirectly. I'm sorry it had to be you, but you were the easiest to target. And that proved to be harder than I hoped." She gave a short bark of laughter and then winced.

"So you faked my death, brought me here. How long will I...Christ, my grandfather! He must think I'm dead. I have to let him know. He's an old man. This could kill him." He moved toward what he had spied as an opening and was blocked by Griff again.

"You don't get it, do you? There's more to this than you remember. Think, Mr. Wolff, think about what happened." She moved to the opening that was being blocked until she moved out. "I have to go out. I'll be back in about an hour."

"Mistress, you should really wait, or let me..." The rest of what Griff said was cut off from the door closing. There was no lock, but he knew that he wouldn't make it very far.

Bradley leaned back against the wall and thought about the last thing he remembered. He'd been at the pack house. His grandparents had walked over from their house for dinner. They were walking around, just talking. He closed his eyes as it washed over him.

"Bradley, my boy, this is the best this house has looked in a coon's age." He and his grandfather were walking around the old gardens. Bradley had just pointed out the new ones that the new cook had insisted on having put in.

"What the hell is a coon's age anyway?" He grinned at the old man. "Yeah, it does look good, doesn't it? Martha is saying that this little project will save the house several hundred dollars a month during the summer months. She said I was to tell you if you pick one tomato, she'll beat you with her broom."

Martha had said more, but he hadn't shared that with his grandda. She hated that he'd pick the biggest green ones for fried green tomatoes. Bradley thought they were nasty tasting when they were ripe, much less green and fried in cornmeal.

"That woman always did have a mean streak. And you tell her I'm not afraid of her old broom. I'll just have your grandma have a little talk with her again," his grandfather groused.

They had walked around some more, ending up on the front porch. That's when David came by, right before supper as always, he remembered now. He and David had fought over escorting their grandmother inside. Good naturedly, of course.

The table had been groaning from the weight of all the food. Martha, even with her taking exception to his grandfather's snitching vegetables, set a great table. He could almost taste the roasted beef and potatoes again. There was green beans and corn on the cob. Plus, she had made homemade noodles, Bradley's favorite. The tea his grandmother made that was so sweet most of the pack shied away from drinking it and given no choice, would dump it in a potted plant or over the rail if they were lucky enough to be outside.

He tensed now, remembering David saying something about Tristan being mated to a woman no one had met. And wondering what kind of person she was. It was said that she was giving him a run for his money, and Aaron was enjoying the hell out of it.

He felt the presence seconds before the creature—he knew it was Griff now—appeared on the table, standing in the middle, growling at everyone there. He had his clawed paws, swiping at anyone who got close enough to try and stop him. Then his hair…someone pulled his hair hard, had grabbed a handful and yanked his head back, exposing his neck. The blade, holy good Christ, she had slit his throat. He felt his blood, warm, running down his chest. He'd tried to hold it, stop the flow, but he was fading fast. The room became fuzzy. He remembered the gun now; he'd heard it at least twice and someone screaming. Then nothing. He knew he had died. She really had killed him.

~~~

She had killed Bradley. Her contract was to kill Bradley, the alpha wolf of the largest pack in the United States. No wonder she thought she wouldn't walk away, every being in the United States was looking for her.

That thought had been circling around Tristan's head for the past three hours and he was no closer to believing it now than he had been when it started.

She had said that she had had no choice. Why? Why didn't she have a choice? And even if she did somehow live through the gunshot wounds, the entire wolf population was out to get her, not to mention every vampire within the realms Aaron knew. That must be what she meant when she said she wouldn't live through this, that she would be killed.

And she had been shot. No one was sure how many times, or where the bullets had entered her. But there was enough blood to indicate that she had taken at least one, maybe as many as two. David had said that she had stepped in front of his gun when he went to fire at this large creature that had come before she killed Bradley.

But Griff was an immortal. The bullets wouldn't hurt him. Maybe weaken him, but not kill him. He sat up. Griff couldn't be weakened, he realized then. Bailey needed him at full strength. Why?

He went to see Mel. He would get answers or else.

"I don't care why you're here, but I want you to go back where you came from. Why I gave you free access it beyond me." He hadn't even spoken yet and Mel was already fussing at him.

"Tell me where she is, Mel. I need to find her. I'm in love with her and I want to find her to tell her." She was in the estate room. Her mother was there too. Tristan knew Bailey needed him, but without her help, he couldn't go to her.

"No, no, no! Damn it, Tristan, didn't you ever hear that word as a child? No!" She was pacing the floor and kept looking at the side door, and now that he noticed, so did her mother.

"I don't remember, damn it. That was nearly forever ago. What's going on?" The door opened and in stepped her father. And the relief was evident on her face.

"Oh thank goodness. Now, Tristan, ask me again." She looked so happy, he nearly missed what she said. "Ask me, damn it!"

"Melody! Was that necessary? Poor man has been through enough. His poor mate is the target of a viscous man hunt. Is it a man hunt when it's a woman? I don't know that I've ever run into that before. I'll have to look it up on the Internet to see if there is a difference in gender hunts." James pulled out a small pad of paper and wrote himself a note before sitting on the sofa.

"Tristan St. James, ask. Me. The. Fucking. Question. And yes, it is necessary. Dad, please, I love you, but please be quiet." She was growling at him, he thought.

"Mel, where is Bailey?" He didn't know why now was any different, but he asked to keep her head from exploding.

"I made a promise not to tell anyone, and I can't break my promise. I can't tell you where Bailey is."

She had put enough emphasis on the word "I" that even a dead man would hear it, he thought, but he was pissed about it all the same. But her staring pointedly at her father had him confused.

"What the fuck? Sorry, ma'am, but what was all that about? You are by and far the most exasperating woman next to Bailey I've ever met. Ask me again, ask me again! I don't..." He had nearly missed what James had said and jerked around to him. "What did you just say?"

"I said that I made no such promises. I can tell you where she is. I assume this is why you asked me to come in here as soon as Tristan came back. Good thinking, my dear. You get that intelligence from my side of the family. Why just the other day I was telling Phillip..."

Tristan put his hand over James' mouth to stem the flow of words. He had been with him before and knew how the man could go on for hours about nothing at all.

"I'm going to remove my hand and you're only going to tell me where she is, all right?" He was staring at him and could see the mirth just brimming to get out. He moved his hand.

"She's in a cave in the Netherlands. A red dragon troll is sheltering her and Bradley until the woman reveals herself." He put his own hand over his mouth this time. He was holding back what Tristan could only assume was either more information, or laughter. He was betting the latter of the two.

"Woman, what woman? The woman! Shit, the hit person. How do we find her?" He was moving a little slow, but was very happy that he was catching up now.

"Ah, Tristan, I'm so very glad you asked. This is something I can tell you." Mel actually rubbed her hands together and Tristan was suddenly afraid.

CHAPTER NINETEEN

Bradley had been pacing the small cave for about two hours now. A lot of things were still unclear, but he was starting to put the pieces together. One thing that he couldn't figure out was why him? He knew why she had killed him, and he shuddered every time he thought about that, but why had he been targeted? Why had he been picked out?

"We are trying to figure that out now. Once the woman who ordered your hit comes forward, then we will know. My mistress wasn't given anything other than you were to die or others would in your place."

Bradley didn't hear him come in. For a big animal, he could move with stealth. "Where is she? Is she all right?" He had been concerned for her health too. He could no longer feel her so he couldn't hear her heart beating either.

"Your host would like to meet you. He wants you to call him Todd. He doesn't really have a name, but he likes the name. So if you would please call him that, several times, it will make him happy." The door behind him opened and there was a horrible smell first, then a large, no, very large troll walked in, a red dragon troll.

"A wolf, ah, she said he would be tasty, but I wasn't to touch, no, not to touch, not even a nibble was I to take. Are you the friend of my Printer, the Printer who plays so well?"

"Hummm, yes, Todd, the Printer is my friend, yes, she is my good friend. Yes." He suddenly felt like Yoda. He looked at Griff when he snorted a laugh.

"My mistress, she said much the same thing the first time she meet Todd too. She also said something about green eggs and ham as well."

"Yes, Dr. Seuss. I remember those stories. I thank you for your hospitality, Todd. I will mention to all I know about you and your accommodations." He remembered enough about trolls to know they were very vain and extremely stupid. He preened, just as Bradley knew he would.

"Where is she? You didn't answer me." He noticed the shake of Griff's head, well, the feathers really, and decided that he didn't want the troll to know.

"The Printer is a good friend to me. She has said that I am the best troll that she had ever known. I will be envied for years to come. First the Printer and now the great alpha. Yes, Todd will be very much envied."

Bradley tried breathing through his mouth and discovered that the smell was now on his taste buds. His belly rolled and he was sure he was going to be sick. Suddenly, he could smell...fresh flowers? Apple pie? Bradley looked over at Griff.

"I would not have you be sick, my lord. Our host would not understand and my mistress would be most embarrassed. You will only smell what gives you most comfort when Todd comes to visit."

Bradley nodded his thanks and continued a conversation with the troll. Once Todd had left and was well out of ear shot, Griff answered him.

"I am to assure you that you will not be harmed in any way. No matter what happens, I am to return you to your family in two day's time." Griff looked back behind him before he continued. "My mistress is dying and if she doesn't feed soon, she will. The bullet wounds are taking their toll on her. Not only has she lost a great deal of blood and will not seek any medical help, but she is suffering from a broken heart. It is most likely that under the current circumstances, someone would expedite her death rather than prevent it anyway. She sent me to you to see if you are in need of anything."

"Griff, why? Why is she willing to die for this? If Aaron knew what the real truth was, he'd do anything to help her."

"Do you think that she would have a chance to explain?" Bradley knew that Griff was correct. "I do not, nor does she. Her grace, the queen, has assured us that she is very close to finding the woman responsible. Once she does, then she is free to tell the reason why my mistress has done what she has done."

"But she'll be dead by then." It wasn't a question of if she would be dead, but more of a statement of fact. "May I see her? I'd like to be with her, even if only to sit next to her."

"Yes, but she is very weak, I'm afraid. She is extremely stubborn and is yet moving about the cave as though she were fit. You will have to go to her, I'm afraid. I have forbidden her to leave the warm room. A fever is taking hold and will take more of her strength than she can give."

"I understand. Yes, of course I'll go to her." Bradley followed the creature. "Griff, can I contact anyone? I would like to contact just one person, one I trust more than anyone I know. Aaron MacManus, he is the master vampire of the realm in which I live."

"You may not speak to anyone other than those in this cave. My mistress is afraid someone will see you and all will be lost. But I believe that we are too far from a town for anyone to see you." Griff hadn't turned around, but led the way to the makeshift stairs. "The part of the cave were my mistress is now is far above here, near the mouth. If you should find a need to get a breath of fresh air after visiting with Todd, then I can allow that. His stench is very...floral. But if you run wolf, I will hunt you down and kill you myself."

"I won't run, and a nice breath of clean air sounds very inviting. I so love North American air." He didn't know where he was really, other than the cave. He hoped that Griff would help him figure it out.

"Then I am sorry to say you will be somewhat disappointed. In the Netherlands, the air is crisper up here in the northern mountains. I wonder how the master here, a Leighton Chalmers, stands such weather. But alas, it is not my home, so I think it should be a nice place to visit."

"Nor do I, Griff, nor do I." Bradley grinned, and felt good for the first time since he woke up.

There was a blazing fire in a pit in her room. The cot where she lay was close to it, and she was wrapped in a blanket. The room smelled of blood and impending death. Bradley was sorry he hadn't come to see her sooner.

Bradley walked to her side and knelt down next to her. Her face was pale and drawn and her hair was wet with sweat. He could hear her heart beating much too slow and she was breathing so faintly that he held his to assure himself he was hearing it. She was indeed very weak.

"I'm sorry." Her voice was faint and weak. And his heart broke for the girl.

"Don't talk, and don't worry about it. I'm fine. I've met my first red dragon troll. Todd. What an odd being he is. He had me rhyming like a character from Dr. Seuss." He held his breath again when she began to cough up blood. "Bailey, let me call your mate for you."

He had figured out that this was Bailey, the mate of Tristan St. James, the one David had been talking about. He wondered what the vamp must be thinking about his mate killing the alpha.

"No, not safe. He'll...she will give him freedom." She tried to roll to her side to look at him, and he moved to help her. He pulled the covers back and was shocked by what was there.

"Bailey, love. Oh God, honey."

She had been shot three times, all in the chest and near dead center. David really was a good shot. Each wound was about an inch apart and just over her right breast. Her blood seeped from each hole. He looked up at her face and saw that she had blacked out. He knew it was now or never and if he didn't hurry, never was very close for her.

He stood up, left the little room, and walked out into the open night. He reached for Sara.

"Sara, bring Tristan St. James to me right now. Tell no one, not even Aaron. I will explain when you get to me."

~~~

Tristan was sitting in the study looking over the list of clues that Mel had given him. Key phrases, she had called them, to help figure out the person who had called his Bailey.

"You can help her by finding the woman responsible for the hit," she'd told him. "Bailey gave me this list and said that these are going to be unique to her. Once we find the 'who,' finding out the 'why' will be fairly easy, Bailey said."

Mel didn't sound too confident, though. She had told him everything she knew about the phone call and the arranged hit on Bradley. He wasn't any closer to finding out where she was than when he had come to the realm, but at least now he was helping to bring her back.

"Is she all right, do you know? I need to know she's coming back to me, Mel. I need to be able to show her how much I love her."

"I don't know, Tristan. I truly don't. She hasn't contacted me, nor has Griff since she left here yesterday morning. She wouldn't even tell me where she was taking him." He could see that she had pissed her off with that.

Tristan had already figured out that Bailey had taken the bullets to keep Griff strong so that he could heal Bradley. He knew without a doubt that she wouldn't kill anyone without good reason. So wherever she was, Bradley was alive. And if Griff had healed Bradley, then he couldn't heal her. She could very well be dying right now.

He looked at the list again and frowned. It wasn't long, just ten words, three phrases. Why? he wondered for the hundredth time. *Why? He* stood and walked over to his makeshift table and started straighten up the pens. He didn't want to think it was possible, but he knew who the woman was who'd ordered the hit. Patrice Skidmore was the one they were looking for.

He picked up his cell phone again and dialed his home in France. He'd almost called four times now and had hung up every time. This time, he let the call go through. The cell phone line that was supposed to be his mother's office rang halfway around the world. He wasn't a mama's boy by any means, but sometimes, like now, one conversation with her could make all the difference.

"Mom, it's Tristan. I need you to come here. I...it's Bailey. She's been hurt, hurt bad. I need your help. Can you come here?"

"Of course you do. How silly of you to think you needed to ask. Your father and I are boarding our plane as we speak. We should be there in about six hours, less if your father will hurry himself along. And I'm bringing my wedding dress. That lovely young woman needs a beautiful wedding, dear. Every woman needs a big wedding and I have it all planned out. She'll love it. Did you want to speak to your father? Trey, here, assure your son things are going to be fine." Tristan smiled. His mother was one in a million, thank goodness.

"Son, things are going to be fine. Your mother says so. Do you need anything else?" His father was not a man of many words, but he did mean every one he uttered.

"No, Dad, just Bailey." Then he realized what she had said. They were getting on the plane now. "How did you know that I needed you to come now? I don't understand. And the dress, why is Mom bringing her...what's going on, Dad?"

"Strange thing, that. Patrice called. Said that you had made a mistake with the stupid cow and that you were going to ask her to marry you very soon. We didn't say anything, of course, but your mother got a bee in her bonnet and off we are to the States." He could hear the concern in his dad's voice and loved him all the more for it. "You didn't make a mistake. You know that, don't you, son?"

"No, no, Dad, I didn't, but Patrice did. I'll explain when you get here, but don't let on to her that we've talked. She's dangerous. I believe she is responsible for Bailey being in the trouble that she's in. And I plan to rectify that as soon as possible."

"All right. She will be fine, Tristan. Bailey is a very strong willed girl. But you'll make her see reason." Tristan smiled and thought that his father had a lot of confidence in his powers of persuasion.

He hung up the phone and turned in the chair to look out at the dark night. The pieces fell into place like a perfect puzzle. Patrice had ordered the hit on the one person she knew would get Bailey killed so she could have Tristan.

Sara came into the room just then, took one look at him, and smiled. "You are so going to love me for this."

CHAPTER TWENTY

Bradley paced across the room again. He had taken off his borrowed shirt and was still sweating. Griff had said that she had had a fever off and on and keeping the room warm would keep her from getting an infection. Bradley didn't say anything as they both knew it was just a matter of time before a fever would be a blessing. She had been tossing and turning for the past hour and she was no longer talking about anything that made sense. The commotion at the mouth of the cave had him turning toward it. The shouts had him smile.

"Bailey? Bailey, where the fuck are you?"

Bradley thought he'd faint with relief. Finally, the troops had arrived. He went to the mouth of the room to show them where the two of them were. He was amazed to see not only Sara and Tristan, but Aaron as well.

"She isn't going to be happy about this. She is going to be really pissed off, as a matter of fact. I said specifically not to..." Bradley said as soon as he saw them. He suddenly couldn't breathe. Aaron had him in such a tight hug that all the wind had been knocked out of him. He could either hug him back or...Bradley hugged his friend. Aaron meant the world to him and he was very glad to see the bloodsucker.

"Aaron, you're killing him, let him go. Besides I want to hug him too." Sara was crying, he noticed. Tears streamed down her cheeks and she had a huge smile on her face. "Come here, fur ball, and give me a hug. Don't you ever scare us like that again, you hear me?"

Bradley looked over Sara's shoulder to see Tristan kissing Bailey. He'd forgotten about that for a moment. He pulled away and walked over to the cot and knelt down on the opposite side of Tristan.

"She's really weak, Tristan." When Tristan looked at Bradley, he could see the anguish in his eyes. "You'll be free as soon as she draws her last breath. You need to decide what you want to do."

Bradley looked over at the vampire. Surely he wasn't thinking about letting her go. This woman had given her life for him, for Bradley too. Had he even thought that the vamp would turn her down, Bradley would have turned her himself. His pack could have used a woman like her.

Sara had knelt beside Tristan as he spoke. "The choice was taken from me the moment I saw her lying in a pool of her own blood all those weeks ago. I'm in love with her, and if she dies or not, I will never be free of her, and I never want to be. I need her more than I need anything in this world." He kissed her hand and tucked it back under the covers. Bradley had held her hand earlier and the coldness of it still bothered him.

"So be it," Sara said with tears in her eyes. "Bailey Morrison St. James, I command you to wake and drink of this man your mate. Wake now, Bailey Morrison St. James."

They all watched as Bailey's eyes fluttered open then closed. Holding their collective breaths, they watched as they opened wide and looked directly at Tristan.

"There you are," she whispered softly. "I love you so much."

Tristan had opened his vein and put his wrist to her mouth. At first they thought she wouldn't sip from him, but as soon as his blood touched her tongue, she drank greedily. Finally after a few minutes, she stopped. Tristan closed the wounds and held her hand. They all watched her, watching for any sign that his blood was healing her.

Sara could only wake her to feed, but couldn't save her. It would be messing with the order of things, the Fates, and she didn't screw around with those broads. What happened now was in the hands of Bailey. And Tristan.

"Will this be enough? Will this heal her?" Tristan looked at Sara. "Is there anything else I can do for her? I need her, Sara. I will not lose her now that I've found her. Tell me what else I can do to save her."

"She needs to believe, Tristan. She needs to know that you're really here and that you'll forgive her for what she's done."

"How? She saw me, talked to…our link. I can talk to her through our link." Tristan smiled.

Everyone left the couple alone as they went to talk to their host and Griff. Bradley introduced them to Todd and told them how much help he'd been in giving them shelter. Bradley thought that Aaron was a brave man for hugging the large troll and when he stepped back, Aaron's eyes were filled with tears. Bradley wasn't sure if it was from emotion or from the stench. Bradley thought it was the latter of the two, especially when Sara declined a hug from her mate.

It was twenty minutes later when Tristan came to find them. He was holding Bailey in his arms and she had her arms wrapped around his neck. Bradley took his first easy breath since he'd awakened hours ago.

"Bailey is…we're going home. She's not going to die and I'm taking her home. I'll…I'll meet you all there." And they disappeared from the room.

Bradley looked at Sara and Aaron. "I'm not letting either of you carry me. She's too small." He pointed at Sara first then at Aaron. "And you stink."

~~~

They all met in the large salon of the mansion at sunset. Tristan had already gone to Bailey and fed her again.

She was much stronger, but still weak, and now staying with Colin and Shade near Becca's Place. She needed a few more days of rest before she would be herself again. Tristan was looking forward to a long life with her and ordered her to stay in bed until this was over. He had also told her he loved her. She had cried, of course, and they had held each other and not said a word for a long time.

Lord and Lady Tristan St. James the Forth arrived just after sunrise. Being older vampires, they were able to tolerate the sun in the early and later hours better than most, and took a leisurely ride in the limo to the estate of the MacManus'. When they arrived with much pomp and circumstance, they were led by a very impressed Duncan to a large suite of rooms in the sublevels of the mansion. Tristan, of course, knew his parents had arrived, just as they knew where he had been. They had been in constant communication since he'd found Bailey. They, too, were now a part of the plan to expose Patrice.

Tristan thought about the conversation that he and Bailey had just had before he left the other mansion. He was telling her everything he knew about the plot to kill Bradley and what people were saying about her. No one other than a select few knew that Bradley was alive, his grandda being one.

Tristan didn't think he would ever forget the look on the older man's face when he'd come face to face with his healthy grandson. Nor the fact that the man kept hugging his grandson to him over and over throughout the time they'd been together.

"She has to die, Tristan. I'm sorry, but that is the way of the realm. She has threatened the lives of not only humans, but non-humans as well. Mel has already imprisoned the others, the weres who helped her." Bailey had her head resting on his chest when she spoke. "Mel is not a cruel leader and will make her death quick and as painless as she is able."

"Yes, I know. But she's been a friend of my family's for centuries. What did she hope to gain from all this? I mean, why Bradley, and why you? I wonder what made her think there was anything between her and me?"

Bailey sat up and looked down at him, confusion all over her face. Shaking her head, she lay back down and held his hand. Her next words stunned him.

"She is in love with being in love with you. No, that's not right. She wanted you. You really are a dumb ass at times, aren't you?" She laughed when he pinched her ass. "Tristan, she thinks that you are hers and you finding me when you did just pushed her over the edge. She's probably thought all her life that you would take her to mate."

"I never gave her any indication that I was...why do you persist in calling me names? Although I think I liked 'sweetums' better than 'dumb ass.' Why can't you come up with names more appropriate? Such as...Long Dick or Sir Long Dick. Doesn't that sound better than—"

She rolled him to his back and straddled him. He reached up and pulled her down to devour her mouth. Had she not been so weak and had he not wanted to get this over with, he'd have gone against the doctor's advice and taken her right there.

"I...tell me you love me again. I've never had anyone tell me that before." She laid her head back on his chest and felt it rumble with laughter.

"You, my love munchkins, are the love of my life and I love you very much." She pounced on him then, smacking him hard against the shoulder.

Now he was sitting in a large room with people, and while he loved most of them, he wanted them gone.

"Earth to Tristan," Patrice snapped at him. "Where are you? You zoned out there for so long we thought you'd gone to sleep. And what is with those ridiculous clothes?"

Patrice had sat down next to him on the large sofa. Tristan looked down at his clothes. He didn't see anything wrong with them. He was actually beginning to like the way they felt. "They're my new style. Colin helped me with them. You don't like the jeans and t-shirt. And this thing, I don't remember what it's called, but it really is soft and comfortable."

The jeans were a pair he had manufactured after a pair Colin had on. Colin had assured him that he wanted to have them worn, not new as they could chaff and "rub ye raw in yer private regions." The t-shirt was like the one Bailey had had on before he'd left her tonight. A depiction of another cartoon character from a show called SpongeBob. This guy was called SquidWorth or some other nonsense. The flannel, he remembered now, was also worn and it actually was hers. Having been too big for her in the first place, it fit him well.

"Well, I don't care for them at all," Patrice told him with a raised brow. "I think you should go change to your other clothes before dinner."

Bossy already, he thought.

"You need to put your suit back on and that lovely tie that I got you for your birthday last year. In fact," Patrice continued. "You should just go do it now before you embarrass us with this ridiculous outfit."

"No." He turned from her before he burst out laughing at the expression on her face. "Mom, how was your vacation in the Everglades? The weather must have been nice."

They had all decided to act as though Bradley was dead until tonight and that there was still a massive manhunt out for Bailey...The Printer. Tristan couldn't wait for the show to begin and loathed acting the happy couple with this person until then. But he was cautioned that she could still be innocent. Without real evidence, they couldn't prove Patrice had anything to do with the plot to kill the alpha even though in his heart, he knew she had.

Tristan looked over at Patrice and winked at her. Her frown at him turned into a smile and she took his hand in hers. With a "we'll talk later about your attire," she settled in next to him.

"Yes, we had a grand time," his mother said with a laugh. "Your father went deep sea fishing. He didn't catch anything, but he had fun, didn't you, dear?"

Tristan was waiting for Aaron's cue. He was tense and ready for this to be over.

"Yes, I had a good time. Tristan," his father said to set things up to capture Patrice, "what can you tell us about the young Bailey we've heard so much about? Someone said that she killed the alpha hereabouts."

CHAPTER TWENTY-ONE

Tristan waited for Aaron. And waited. Tristan looked over at him and wasn't really surprised to see him wrapped up in his mate. Sara and he couldn't seem to keep their hands off each other. Tristan couldn't wait to get to Bailey and do the same thing.

He reached out to him and, none too gently, reminded him of his part in this play. "Would you mind paying attention? I would very much like to go to Bailey and do what you're doing to Sara, but I CAN'T IF YOU DON'T HELP!" He grinned when Aaron jumped slightly.

"I'm sorry. Did you say something about Bailey? She's supposed to come by later and we're going to talk about what happened at the pack house the other day." He looked around the room in general as he spoke.

"She's coming here?" Patrice squeaked out. "But I thought...here? Are you sure about that? I mean, there isn't any reason for her to come here, is there? Why? Isn't she, like, wanted for murder or something?"

"Well, she said that she had proof that she was tricked into killing him and she was going to share it with me. I can't imagine what it could be, but she has a good reputation as a hired killer and I, for one, am willing to see what she has. The queen said that I should give her a listen and for as much as Mel can be an irritant, she is the queen. Bailey may have something that would clear her name. Proof is all it takes and she said she had plenty of it." Aaron coolly sat back in his chair.

"Proof. She doesn't have any proof." Patrice looked around the room. "I mean, what kind of proof could she have? And besides, someone said that she'd been shot. Maybe she's already dead like that poor wolf. I don't think this is such a good idea, Aaron. You should tell the authorities that she's…can't you get into trouble for harboring a criminal?"

Tristan sitting next to her and saw her fidget and tense up. She was nervous, he thought. Good. When she started to pace, he watched her closely. He didn't trust her not to do something stupid. He'd go along with this to a point, but he didn't want anyone else hurt either.

"Oh, didn't you hear?" Aaron grinned hugely as he continued. "Bradley isn't dead. Bailey turned him over to the queen this morning. She had only made it look like he was dead so she could expose whoever set up the hit on him. He is in very good health, if only a little tired. Bailey had him hidden somewhere and now she's ready to come forward. I would think that alone is proof enough. Can you image what she would have had to have gone through to fake his death? Scary to think about."

"No, no that's not right. He's dead. He has to be. We had a deal. I would let the others live, but she had to die. No, you're wrong." Patrice started pacing the floor. "She reneged on her end of our bargain. I told her he had to die or I would expose her. This wasn't a part of the deal."

"What kind of deal? What are you talking about?" Sara asked. "What do you know about this whole thing, Patrice?"

Tristan leaned back and let her go. He could sense the others in the room now, many men and Mel. They were there to keep the others safe in case Patrice tried something else.

"I have information that says she's killed others. Many others, and not just our kind but humans too, cold blooded murder. She's taken money. Why, she even had her brother killed to make more money. You should just kill her as soon as she gets here, Mr. MacManus. She's dangerous. I…I know, I've seen the paperwork myself." Everyone watched her. Patrice was unraveling the more she spoke.

"Information? What sort of information? She mentioned that she had paperwork too." Aaron stood in front of her now. "What is it you know, Patrice? Something about this plot you're not telling me? As master of this realm, I must insist that you tell me all you know about Bailey."

Tristan had never heard Aaron use that tone before. It was a compelling tone, one that any vampire who wasn't as strong as him must obey.

"No, I can't…stop. Please stop. Don't make me." Her voice had turned pleading now, begging and whinny.

"Patrice Skidmore, Lady Skidmore of the Royal House of Vampirism, I command that you speak the truth.

You will tell me all you know about the woman Bailey Morrison St. James, also known as the Printer. Now!"

Tristan watched the entire room shift in their seats. Patrice couldn't disobey the compulsion now. It lay heavy in the room. Curiously, he didn't feel it, and looked around the room. Even his father seemed to be feeling the effects of it.

"She's not his mate. I am. I'm his mate. Tristan is mine. She is supposed to be dead. They were to kill her. I had that stupid cop show up with his gun loaded with silver to kill her. And he couldn't even do that right, stupid Barney Fife fool. I've watched for years, waiting and collecting. Gathering information so she would have to kill him. I'd give her no choice. What good is a single wolf anyway, not even mated? How is he...he can't pass on his little kingdom without an heir. They should be thanking me. Thanking me." Spittle flew from Patrice's mouth as she ranted. No one said a word when she started to pace again.

"She wouldn't even kill those brats of yours." She screamed at Sara. "I told her to, told her to take them both out or else. What did she do? She told me that she'd hunt me down and make my death slow and painful if I touched them. I believed her, too. She is just crazy enough to try and kill me. Like she could even get close to me once Tristan and I mated. He'll protect me, won't you? You'd never let her hurt me, would you?"

When she came toward him, Tristan backed away. Patrice was insane. Not only that, but had been for a long while. Why hadn't anyone ever seen it before?

"She's a nothing anyway, not even able to get with child. We'd bred that right out of her when she was in our lab. I told them that she needed to be destroyed, all those failures. She was as useless then as she is now. We never did figure out how she got the others out. Sneaky little bitch. And then that fool stepped in front of my bullet when I tried to kill her myself. She actually blew my lab up, her and those others. Well, I took something from her too, didn't I? had that Salvatore kill that fag brother of hers."

No one moved when she sat back down. No one said a word. Patrice had just admitted to more than planning the plot to kill Bradley and destroy Bailey. She had admitted to killing perhaps hundreds of others inside the lab, where horrific things had been done in the name of science and technology.

"So you were a part of the lab," Bailey said in a soft voice. "Griff said you were, but I didn't want to believe him. You're quite mad, do you know that? And if the queen doesn't kill you, I will take great pleasure in it."

Tristan looked over to where Bailey was standing. He hadn't even felt her come in the room. Mel was just behind her, as were Colin, Dominic, and Bradley.

"You're supposed to be dead," Patrice said softly to Bailey. "I'm going to make sure that once I'm married to Tristan, you are hung from our front door until the crows pick you clean. Aren't we, love? We will make sure that she never bothers us again."

Patrice leaned over and put her head on Tristan's shoulder. He felt a shudder of complete revulsion slam through his body. He decided that he couldn't let this…animal touch him again. He stood and walked over to his beloved.

Bailey looked pale and drawn. She shouldn't be here, he thought, but then maybe she should, too. She deserved knowing as much as the rest of the people in the room.

"It was you, wasn't it? You were the one who bred us, the egg used to make me. That's why I couldn't read you in the building, why I couldn't harm you that day. You fixed it so that I couldn't harm you." Bailey staggered slightly and would have fallen had Tristan not grabbed her. Tristan turned to stare at Patrice again with her in his arms. He laid her gently on the couch well away from Patrice.

"Yes, I'm your mommy. Don't you just love a happy ending?" Patrice pulled out a gun and shot Abby St. James.

"Mother!" Tristan ran to his mother and clutched her body to his.

His father had grabbed Patrice and snapped her neck before she could take her next breath. He looked over at Aaron and they all watched as he pulled a sword from off the fireplace mantel and while Trey held her up by the hair, Aaron sliced her head from her shoulders. Patrice Skidmore was truly dead.

"Move," Bailey said with authority in her voice. "Let me have her. Tristan, remove your hand."

His mother, his dear mother, was bleeding to death and someone was trying to take her from him. He finally focused when someone slapped him hard across the face. Bailey.

"Tristan, I need for you to let her go to Bailey. She can't help her if you're holding her." Mel was speaking to him now. He looked at her. Nothing was going through the fog he had in his head.

"Son, let me have her. Let me have your mom." It was his dad, his dad needing her that had him letting go. "Go to work, girl. Don't let her die. I need her." Tristan watched as he handed his mother over to Bailey.

Bailey looked up at him, then at the senior St. James. She looked nervous and scared. She looked beautiful to him.

"You must ask me, sir. And then I must have a boon. It must be worthy of this life you ask me to save. It must be worthy of your love for her."

"I ask for her life, for she is my all. I ask for her life so that I may live to see my children love her again. For your boon, I give to you my son. His love for you is worthy of my love for her. Take him and his love in return for mine." He kissed Bailey's forehead and relinquished his hold on his mate.

"I accept your boon and your request. Now, all of you back the fuck up and let me work. I can't do this with you all breathing down my neck."

His father snorted. "Just like a woman."

Bailey quickly moved her hands along the wound that hemorrhaged away the life of his mother. He watched as they began to glow to a blinding white then a hue so red it washed out the blood staining his mother's blouse. In a matter of seconds, he saw that her breathing had become less labored and the blood less copious. When she moved her head to look at his dad, his legs buckled beneath him and he dropped to the floor. The kiss they shared was one of the most romantic things he had ever witnessed. Bailey was healing his mother.

It was another few minutes before she finished, and several more before she moved back away from her. Tristan picked her up. He could see that what she had done had completely depleted her strength. Cradling her in his arms, he looked over at his parents. They didn't seem to notice anyone but each other. He stood to leave.

"She will need to sleep for several hours, Tristan. And then she will need you and what you can give her. Take her back to Colin's house. There is more to be done yet. She will need to rest." Mel was leading him to the door where Colin and Aaron still stood.

"When she is better, we will need to sit down and talk, you and me." Tristan only nodded at Aaron, his total focus on the woman in his arms.

The trip to her room at the Larimore home took only seconds. He put her into her unmade bed and covered her up with the quilts. After making sure that the room was secure, he lit a few candles in the room and lay down beside her.

He couldn't remember his life before her, knowing only that she was the reason he wanted to live. His plans from the first time he lay beside her to now were so different that had he thought about it, he would have been very surprised at his own arrogance back then. Now, all he could think about was making her happy and safe. He didn't think about the talk that Aaron wanted to have with him, nor the fact that his father had just killed a childhood friend right in front of witnesses. His total focus was on Bailey.

CHAPTER TWENTY-TWO

"How you feeling today?"

Bailey had been napping again. She hated that every time someone had come in the room over the past two days she'd been asleep. Shade had come to see her twice a day and woke her both times.

"Better. I'm sorry. You must think I'm a slug or something. I don't normally sleep this long. I feel ridiculous." She began fussing with the covers.

"Oh gee, you think? Hummm, I was thinking more along the lines of a wood sloth. You have been such a nuisance." Then she smiled at her. "Get real, you've been shot three times, saved the alpha and a woman you've never met, bringing her back from certain death. I think if anyone needs to rest, it is certainly you."

Bailey felt her face flame with embarrassment. Shade sat down on the bed beside her. She just noticed that she had a bundle in her arms. It looked like a load of laundry.

"I'm being stupid again, aren't I? Tristan told me that I should be resting more. But I don't know how that would be possible."

"You've gone through a great deal. I think if anyone deserves to rest, it's you." Shade looked down at the laundry. "There was a trial for Patrice. She was found guilty of treason and murder. It sounds silly, but she was sentenced to death. How do you put a dead person to death?"

"They had to, Tristan said. Or his father and Aaron could be put into prison for a century for killing one of their own. It's a way to prove that not only was Patrice a murderer, but that they were justified in killing her." Bailey leaned back against the headboard before going on. "Abby said that in the old days when a vamp went rogue, they simply staked them in the sun for two days. If they were not guilty then the elders said they would live. Stupid as that sounds, they really believed it."

"I'm glad for the council then. There is also talk of you being made a member of the pack. Honorary, of course. Bradley had a meeting with his entire pack and told them that you not only saved his life, but that of several members of his pack as well. He told them about a troll named Todd also."

Bailey laughed. She wondered if Todd the dragon troll would thank her for his fame, or would he wish he'd never helped her at all? She thought Todd would love it. He would be telling his friends that he had helped the great Printer, yes, the Printer he had helped.

"Todd was a good guy. Someday I'll have to take you to meet him. He could read some children's rhymes for you."

Both women laughed and suddenly, Shade stood up. She looked nervous. But before Bailey could ask her what was going on, she started out of the room. She dropped her laundry on the bed and shot out of the room.

"I have…I have to run downstairs for a minute. I have something on the…I'm making you soup for lunch. I was wondering if…could you keep an eye on this for me?"

Before she was ten feet from the door, the bundle started crying.

"What the fuck? Hey, Shade! *Shade, get your ass back here!"* She poked at the bundle and it cried harder. "Damn it, Shade, this isn't funny."

"Pick it up." Tristan had come into the room, but she couldn't hear a word he was saying over the din from the blanket. "Bailey, just pick it up."

"What the hell is this thing? And why the hell would it cry? I didn't do anything to it. It probably wants Shade to come back and get it." She poked at it again. "What am I supposed to do with it?" She figured out it was a baby, but a baby what she didn't have a clue.

"Pick it up." He had enunciated each word like she was stupid.

Well, she supposed she was. She knew *nothing* about babies in any form or creature. She reached down and grabbed the blanket it was wrapped in and held it up with one hand.

"Christ, Bailey, not like that. You want to hurt her?" He had flashed across the room and took the bundle from her, thank goodness.

"I didn't do anything to it. Shade just dropped that thing off and took off out of here like she'd been shot from a cannon. Then it started screaming. No one can blame me for that." She was frustrated, but the thing had finally shut up. "How did you get it to shut up?"

"I'm holding her like a baby and not a weapon. You probably scared it yelling like that. Don't you know anything about babies?"

He was rocking back and forth now. She didn't know why that would be comforting to anyone. It was making her car sick just watching him.

"I didn't even know what it was until you said it was a baby. She's lucky I didn't kick it off the end of the bed when she left. I thought it was laundry or something. Who would leave a kid with me? And no, I have no clue what to do with one of them. That's the first one I've ever seen this close."

He looked at her strangely, but she was too embarrassed to try and figure out why. She leaned back on the bed and watched him. He seemed to know what he was doing anyway.

"Here, take her. Put your arms like this and I'll put her in your arms for you." She looked at him, her eyes wide as she could make them.

"Are you insane? Take it? No fu...friggin' way. That thing hates me. Keep it away from me, Tristan, or so help me, when I can, I'll hurt you." She was backing as far away as she could, which wasn't far because he had sat on the bed in front of her and on top of the blankets.

"It's not an 'it,' she's a baby. A little baby girl. Now put your hand out and take her. You scared her and you need to make it up to her."

"I scared her? She's the one who started screaming like I was cutting her leg off or something. Please don't, I can't hold her. What if I drop her or something?" It was no use, she thought. She either took it from him or crawled up the headboard and over the top.

He dropped the bundle in her arms. Well, he didn't drop, she thought, so much as gently placed it in her arms. It was lighter than she thought it would be, but squirmy and limp. She held it stiff armed away from her. She looked up at Tristan. She was terrified he would leave her with it.

"Now what? Look, Tristan, it's puckering up again. Take it!" She tried to shove it back at him, but he moved away from her. Not too far, she noticed, but far enough away she couldn't just toss it back.

"Stop calling her an it. And she's puckering up because you're holding her like a sack of flour. Cuddle her to you, like this. That's it, now relax."

"Relax? This is a kid and it hates me. What if I drop it or something? They'll all blame me for it and I didn't even want the thing." She tried cuddling it close, but it looked ready to scream again. "Tristan, help me, take it…her, please?" She knew she was begging, and whinny, but she was terrified.

"You're in bed, honey. The only thing that will happen if you drop her is you'll piss her off again. And you don't need to have the death grip on her. She won't fall out of your arms. That's it. You're getting the hang of it." He was lying down at the foot of the bed now, looking like he didn't have a care in the world. *Dirty bastard,* she thought.

"Okay, now take her. I held her, she's not crying, I've made up. Take her back." She moved forward to give her to him when the kid looked all tense again. Bailey leaned back on the headboard again and she looked fine. She glared at Tristan.

"What? She likes where she's at. I didn't put her up to it," he told her as she glared harder.

Bailey looked down at the baby in her arms for the first time. She had a pretty face, she thought, and tons of black, shiny hair. She looked at Tristan, the unspoken question hanging between them.

"No, love, she isn't mine. But thank you for thinking I'd be so callous as to do this to you like this." He looked wounded and she felt bad about it. She hadn't meant to think that, but he'd been so pushy about her to hold it, err, her.

"I'm sorry. But I don't know anything about this. Shade comes in here and drops off a bundle of laundry that starts screaming and then suddenly, you show up all pushy and knowing what to do." She looked down at her again and wondered if her cheeks were as soft as they looked. The kid kept staring at her and it was a little nerve wracking.

"Most of my brothers have children. Phil has two daughters and Mark had three sons. My oldest brother Daniel has six, three of each, and three grandchildren, all girls. My brother Aiden is the only one who isn't mated, and I doubt he'll ever settle down enough to let a woman love him. I've been around children for a long time. I'm sorry about being pushy, but I was surprised how scared you looked and I wanted to show off. I'm sorry, baby." He did look sorry, she thought.

"Why does she stare at me like that? I can't be that ugly, can I?"

Finally giving into temptation, she swept her finger gently down her cheek. She'd been wrong; her skin was much softer than it looked.

"You aren't the least bit ugly; you are by far the most beautiful woman I've ever seen. And she stares because you are no longer shouting at her, and you've finally relaxed enough to not squeeze the life out of her."

Bailey barely heard him. The little girl was puckering her little pink lips again, but not in a cry, but like she was sucking on something. "What's she doing?" She just noticed that her voice had lowered and that she was leaning back, cradling her close to her. She suddenly didn't care. She reached up to touch her again and the baby grabbed her finger. She jerked her eyes to Tristan.

"Its okay, love. She trusts you, that's all. She looks like she might be hungry. Shade probably went to get her a bottle." He sat up now and moved behind Bailey, settling himself behind her and her cupped between his legs. She leaned back on his chest and when he put his arm under hers to hold the little girl too, she relaxed even more.

"Tristan, I...I'm so sorry, but...you heard Patrice. I can't have children. I'm sure you want some, but...I'm not able to have them. Please take her now. I'm really tired."

She suddenly hurt more than she'd ever hurt. She wouldn't be able to give Tristan one of these beautiful precious babies of his own. And holding this one hurt her too. She had fallen in love with this little girl the moment she'd touched her cheek. She wanted to crawl into a hole and cry for the unfairness of it.

"You're right, Bailey. I want to raise lots of children. Many, many children with you." She burst into tears anyway, not even waiting for him to leave the room this time.

~~~

They had taken a chance with this. He knew this and he hated doing it. But Bailey was his life and he did want children with her. This one, this little girl.

Mel had told him that the Fates had informed her that he and Bailey were to raise a great child, that the child would be the one who brought the humans and the other beings together in such a way that it would mean greater things for all beings. And through their love, her strength and his mind, many children would be loved and cared for over the ensuing years.

Tristan held Bailey to him, comforting and soothing her. She was hurting and he had been the cause of it, he thought. He wanted to fix it, but he also feared that if told her that they were destined to care for the lost children, she would balk. That's why they had come up with the plan to have her fall in love with a child and then ask her.

The little girl, who was probably about two to three months old, was of vampire descent, more than likely a pure blood. Someone had found her strapped into a car seat in an open field yesterday afternoon. Her parents, or as best they could tell, had been staked to the ground and left to meet the sun. There was nothing left to make a positive identification of them or the baby. Presumably, whoever had killed her parents thought that the little girl would meet the same fate. But children of vampires, pure or not, did not pick up the traits of vampirism until they were in their late twenties. Someone had dropped her off at Becca's Place today, starving and cold.

Bailey moved back more and looked at Tristan. He marveled everyday that she was his. She had saved his mother's life, and his. His mother was, at this moment, planning a huge wedding ceremony for them.

"You could have just asked, you know?" The baby was asleep now, her little fist stuck in her mouth.

He started to ask her what she meant, but he didn't. What would be the point? They both knew what he should have done.

"What would you have said if I'd brought the baby in here and said I want us to adopt her? You were terrified of her as it was." He ran his finger down Bailey's cheek, and then he touched the baby's.

"Hummm, I'm not sure. Told you to fu...frig off, I suppose." She laid the baby on the bed and turned her in her arms to be held. "Why do I do that, change my language for her? She can't understand a word I say."

"Bailey, I love you. I don't know, I think it's instinct, maybe. My brothers all did the same thing. Even I do it when they're around. We should talk about this. Plus, hummm, you should know that...Bailey, my mom is planning a wedding for us."

"I know. She came in today and had me try on her dress. Said it wouldn't do. I don't know what she meant, but she went out shaking her head and muttering something about my breasts. Your father, he is...I like him. He makes me feel good about myself."

He would, Tristan thought. "He told me he loves you. Said of all his daughters-in-law, you were by far his newest. But he did tell me that you would forever hold a special place in his heart for saving his mate and my brother...well, I don't think you'll ever want for bodyguards as long as they're around. Aiden is quiet smitten with you already. I've warned him off. He's the ladies man of the family."

"His newest, huh?" Bailey looked at the sleeping baby. "I'm not sure about all this. I don't do well with people, you know, and what about her? About the baby...do you know her name?" Bailey touched her again, but left her to sleep on the bed.

"No, someone killed her parents, and tried to kill her too. She is only a couple of months old. I'm not sure we'll ever be able to figure out who her family is. But I want her to be with us, Bailey. I would like for you and me to raise her."

Bailey didn't say anything for a long while, just stared at the baby. He couldn't see her face as she stared at the baby, but he could feel her relaxed against him. When she looked back at him, his breath caught at the smile on her mouth.

"I would like to raise her with you too. But you have to know, if she wants to be girly, she's going back to live with Shade."

He laughed. "What should we call her?"

"Emma. Emma St. James."

ABOUT THE AUTHOR

I woke up one morning and decided to give play time to the people in my head who were keeping me awake. Little did I know that they would be so relentless and want their time right now! I wrote for the pure joy of it and to entertain my family and friends. But mostly it was to get more than an hour of sleep without a story playing out. Of course, the more I write, the more they want. So...well, as a result of sleepless days (I work through the night as a gun toting grandma – nope not a vigilantly but an armed security guard) I have lots of stories written.

Hello! My name is Kathi Barton and I'm an author. I have been married to my very best friend Sonny for at times seems several lifetimes – in a good way, honey. And together we have three wonderful children and then the ones we brought into the world - Paul and Dale Barton, Jason and Wendy Barton and Danielle and Ben Conklin. They have given us seven of the greatest treasures on Earth. They don't live at home seven days a week! No, seriously, seven grandchildren – Gavin, Spring, Ben, Trinity, Sarah, Kelly and Kian.